IDE.

Rahul

Best Souvie

Ever

This is a work of fiction. Similarities to real people, places, or events are entirely coincidental.

IDENTITY ZERO

First edition. April 27, 2024.

Copyright © 2024 Brian Leslie.

ISBN: 979-8224098729

Written by Brian Leslie.

Table of Contents

INTRODUCTION 1
CHAPTER 1 4
CHAPTER 2 18
CHAPTER 3 31
CHAPTER 4 44
CHAPTER 5 57
CHAPTER 6 77
CHAPTER 7 91
CHAPTER 8 107
CHAPTER 9 123
CHAPTER 10 144

INTRODUCTION

The sweltering Nevada desert stretched endlessly in every direction, the scorching sun beating down mercilessly on the lonely desert highway. Nick and Sandra Harris, along with their teenage son Jamie, were making the long drive from Chicago to Los Angeles for a summer vacation. Little did they know the harrowing nightmare that awaited them.

After hours on the road, they stopped for a bite at a nondescript roadside diner in the middle of nowhere. Jamie opted to stay in the car, bobbing his head to music on his headphones while his parents went inside. When they returned, their son had vanished without a trace. A cold dread gripped Nick and Sandra's hearts as they frantically searched the diner and parking lot. But Jamie was simply gone, seeming to have vanished into thin air.

Frantic, they contacted the local sheriff's department in the small town of Elk County. But Nick immediately sensed something amiss with the sheriff's nonchalant questioning and seeming lack of urgency. Digging deeper, they discovered that two other boys, Jamie's age, had gone missing in recent months; their bodies were eventually discovered far out in the desert.

A seasoned detective named Rachel Valdez from Las Vegas, who initially investigated the two boys' deaths, was originally skeptical of Nick's concerns about the sheriff's potential involvement. However, everything changed when a crucial piece of evidence turned up - a scrap of Jamie's clothing stuck in the trunk liner of the sheriff's patrol car.

The stakes were raised as it became terrifyingly clear that Jamie's life hung in the balance, the twisted sheriff holding him captive somewhere. A race against time ensued as Detective Valdez and the Harris family scoured the desert for any clues to Jamie's whereabouts. The Harris's holed up in a seedy desert motel, fearing the worst with every passing hour.

The tension reached a fever pitch when Valdez traced the sheriff's truck tracks to a remote abandoned mine shaft in the desert. In a climactic showdown, she stumbled upon the deranged sheriff preparing to brutally end Jamie's life. Gunshots rang out as Valdez risked everything to save the young boy.

In the final heart-pounding moments, Jamie was rescued, but not before a harrowing fight for his life. The reunited Harris family embraced amid tears of joy and relief, though shaken to their core. While Jamie's life was spared, the imprints of his horrific desert captivity would never leave him.

.

Detective Valdez's tenacious investigation and the Harris family's unwavering determination had ultimately prevailed against a sadistic killer lurking in the unlikeliest of places. Their harrowing desert odyssey was finally over, but the scars would linger as reminders of how swiftly an idyllic family road trip can take an utterly chilling turn into the nightmarish heart of darkness.

CHAPTER 1

The morning sun shimmered off the windshield as Nick Harris stood back to admire their fully-loaded SUV. Sandra appeared at his side, her long wavy brown hair cascading over a floral summer dress. With a warm smile, she wrapped her arm around her husband's waist.

"Looks like we're all set," she said, excitement radiating from her voice. "This is going to be one amazing vacation."

"Absolutely," Nick agreed, his strong jawline tightening with determination and enthusiasm. "We've earned this."

From the open garage, Jamie emerged, headphones already on and bobbing his head to his favorite tunes. He shot an enthusiastic thumbs-up to his parents, his blond curls bouncing with every step.

"Hey, buddy," Nick called out, pulling Jamie into a playful headlock. "Ready for the adventure of a lifetime?"

"Totally!" Jamie grinned, extricating himself from his father's grasp. "I can't wait to hit the road!"

With one final check of their belongings, the Harris family piled into the car and embarked on their summer vacation. Their spirits soared as they cruised along the open highway, leaving behind the familiar comforts of home in search of new experiences and lasting memories.

"First stop, Grand Canyon!" Nick announced, drumming his fingers on the steering wheel in rhythm with the music blasting from the car stereo.

"Then Vegas, baby!" Sandra chimed in, her eyes sparkling with anticipation. "Remember the last time we were there, Nick?"

"Of course," he replied, chuckling. "How could I forget our little 'adventure' at the roulette table?"

As they reminisced, miles of sweltering Nevada desert stretched out before them. The scorching sun hung mercilessly in the sky, casting its oppressive heat over the arid landscape. Despite the harsh environment, the family was undeterred, the thrill of their road trip fueling their excitement.

"Mom, do you think we'll see any cool desert animals?" Jamie asked, peering out the window at the vast expanse of sand and scrub.

"Maybe," Sandra replied thoughtfully. "Just keep your eyes peeled and who knows what we might spot."

"Like a rattlesnake or a coyote!" Jamie added, his imagination running wild with possibilities.

"Or a roadrunner," Nick interjected with a grin. "But let's hope Wile E. Coyote isn't too far behind."

The three of them laughed, their spirits lifted by the camaraderie and anticipation of what lay ahead. As the endless desert continued to unfold before them, the Harris family embraced their adventure, eager to discover the thrill and wonder that awaited them on the open road.

A shimmering mirage seemed to dance on the horizon, teasing the eye with its elusive beauty. Nick squinted at the sight, mentally calculating the distance to the next town. They'd been driving for hours now, and the desolate expanse of desert was beginning to wear on them.

"Look!" Sandra exclaimed suddenly, pointing to a speck in the distance. "Is that...?"

"Could be," Nick replied, his voice tinged with hope. "Let's find out."

As they drew closer, the nondescript building materialized from the heat haze like a lone oasis in the harsh desert landscape. A weathered sign announced their salvation: "Maggie's Diner – Food, Gas, Cold

Drinks." Relief washed over the family as they pulled into the gravel parking lot.

"Alright, everyone out!" Nick commanded, unbuckling his seatbelt. "Time for a pit stop."

"Actually, Dad..." Jamie hesitated, tapping his headphones. "I'm really into this album right now. Maybe I could stay here and listen while you guys grab something to eat?"

"Are you sure, kiddo?" Sandra asked, concerned. "You haven't had anything since breakfast."

Jamie nodded, his eyes alight with excitement. "Yeah, I'm good. I'll just hang out here with my music."

"Alright," Nick acquiesced, casting a wary glance at the seemingly empty landscape. "But if you need anything, don't hesitate to come inside and find us, okay?"

"Got it, Dad. Thanks!" Jamie flashed a grateful smile, sinking back into his seat and immersing himself in the world of his favorite tunes.

As Nick and Sandra exited the car, they shared a brief, worried look before heading toward the diner. The door creaked open, admitting them into the cool interior and the promise of sustenance. Unbeknownst to them, the oasis they had stumbled upon would soon become the epicenter of a nightmare that would test the limits of their courage, love, and determination.

The diner's overhead fan whirred lazily, offering little relief from the heat but setting the scene for a quintessential desert pit stop. The flickering neon sign cast an eerie glow on the small booths lining the walls, and the smell of greasy comfort food filled the air. Nick and Sandra slid into one of the vinyl seats, their fingers still sticky with sweat.

"Nothing like a good old-fashioned American diner," Nick said, his voice tinged with excitement as he picked up the laminated menu.

"Absolutely," Sandra agreed, her eyes sparkling as she skimmed over the options. "These places always have the best milkshakes."

"Speaking of which," Nick began, catching the attention of a waitress with a quick wave, "two chocolate milkshakes, please."

"Coming right up," the waitress replied with a smile.

"Can you believe we're finally on vacation?" Sandra asked, leaning in close to Nick. "I can't wait to explore the national parks and see the Grand Canyon."

"Me neither, babe," Nick responded enthusiastically. "Jamie's going to love it too. I just hope he doesn't get too attached to those headphones of his."

Sandra chuckled softly. "He's just at that age where music is everything. Remember when we were like that?"

"True," Nick conceded, smiling at the memory. "Alright, let's order some food and then hit the road again."

They dove into conversation about the various sights they planned to visit, their voices filled with anticipation. As they enjoyed their meal, time seemed to slip away unnoticed. It wasn't until the plates were cleared and the last drops of their milkshakes consumed that they glanced at the clock on the wall.

"Wow, we've been here longer than I thought," Nick admitted, concern creeping into his voice. "We should check on Jamie."

"Agreed," Sandra said, her brow furrowing. "I hope he's not bored out of his mind."

They paid the bill and made their way back to the car, the gravel crunching beneath their feet. As they approached, it was immediately clear that something was off. The car door stood ajar, and Jamie was nowhere to be seen.

"Jamie?" Nick called out, his voice strained as he peered into the empty vehicle. "Buddy?"

"Where could he have gone?" Sandra asked, panic rising in her chest as she scanned the desolate landscape.

"Maybe he went inside while we were eating," Nick suggested, though the uncertainty in his eyes betrayed his doubt.

"Let's go check," Sandra urged, grabbing Nick's hand and leading him back to the diner.

As they retraced their steps, their minds raced with worry, each lost in their own thoughts but united in their growing desperation to find their son.

Nick's heart pounded in his ears as he and Sandra burst back into the diner, their eyes darting around the room in frantic search of their son.

The clatter of dishes and laughter from patrons filled the air, but all they could hear was the echo of Jamie's name as they called out for him.

"Jamie!" Sandra shouted, her voice cracking with fear.

"Hey, has anyone seen a teenage boy? Blonde hair, headphones?" Nick asked, desperation lacing his words.

The other patrons exchanged uneasy glances before shaking their heads, their own conversations silenced by the Harris's distress.

"Damn it, where is he?" Nick muttered under his breath, running a hand through his dark hair, frustration and worry etching lines across his face.

"Nick, we need to keep looking," Sandra said, her voice quivering as she gripped her husband's arm tightly.

"Excuse me," a gravelly voice interjected. They turned to find Maggie Johnson, the owner of the diner, concern carved into the wrinkles of her tanned face. "I couldn't help but overhear. What's going on?"

"Our son, Jamie. He was waiting in the car while we ate, and now he's gone," Sandra explained, tears welling up in her eyes.

"Headphones, you said?" Maggie inquired, a thoughtful expression clouding her features. "I think I saw him earlier, walking toward the restroom."

"Thank you," Nick said, nodding gratefully at Maggie's information. "We'll go check there."

"Let me know if you need any more help," Maggie offered, her eyes filled with sympathy as she watched the couple hurry towards the restrooms.

Nick's mind raced as they searched, each unanswered call for Jamie driving another nail into the coffin of panic that threatened to consume him. _Where are you, buddy?_ he thought, struggling to keep his emotions in check for Sandra's sake.

"Stay strong, Nick. We'll find him," Sandra whispered, as if reading his thoughts. Together, they continued their frantic search, the weight of uncertainty and fear growing heavier with each passing moment.

Nick's heart pounded in his chest as they stepped out of the diner, the scorching desert heat washing over them like a suffocating blanket. He squinted against the sun, scouring the dusty parking lot for any sign of Jamie. "Let's split up," he suggested to Sandra, hoping that covering more ground would increase their chances of finding their son.

"Good idea," Sandra agreed, her eyes shining with determination despite the fear that gripped her heart. "I'll check behind the diner and that old gas station."

"Alright. I'll search around the cars and see if anyone else has seen him," Nick replied, already striding towards a group of people who had just exited the diner.

"Jamie!" he called out, his voice cracking with desperation. "Can anyone help us? Our son is missing. He's 14, blonde hair, about this tall," he gestured, trying to remain composed as concern furrowed the brows of the strangers.

"Sorry, man. We didn't see anyone like that," one of them replied sympathetically, shaking his head.

"Thanks anyway," Nick muttered, moving on to another car, his heart sinking further with each fruitless encounter.

"Any luck?" Sandra asked, reappearing at his side, her face flushed from running in the oppressive heat.

"Nothing," Nick admitted, frustration simmering beneath his worry. "What about you?"

"Same," she sighed, her voice thick with emotion. "I don't understand. Where could he have gone?"

"Okay, let's think," Nick said, forcing himself to stay rational amidst the chaos. "If he wandered off to explore or something, where would he go?"

"Towards the highway, maybe?" Sandra offered, her gaze flickering in that direction. "Or the hills behind the diner?"

"Right. Let's check both. You take the hills, and I'll head for the highway," Nick decided, his voice firm despite the churning fear that threatened to overwhelm him.

"Alright. Be careful," Sandra warned, her eyes searching his for reassurance.

"Always," he promised, giving her a quick kiss before they separated once more, both praying that their search would finally bring Jamie back to them.

As the sun began its slow descent towards the horizon, painting the sky with streaks of red and gold, the barren landscape seemed to mock their efforts, offering no trace of their missing son. The oppressive heat felt like a physical weight pressing down on Nick's chest, his heart heavy with dread as each passing moment brought only more uncertainty and despair.

Nick's boots crunched on the gravel as he stared at the empty highway, his heart pounding with frustration and fear. Sandra returned from the hills, her eyes red-rimmed and her hands trembling. Their desperate search had yielded nothing, no sign of Jamie at all.

"Nick," Sandra gasped, breathless. "We can't find him. What do we do now?"

He clenched his jaw, every fiber of his being urging him to keep searching, but he knew they needed help. "We have to call the sheriff's department. Maybe they've seen him or someone brought him in."

"Okay," she nodded, wiping away tears threatening to spill. "Let's do it. The sooner, the better."

As they walked back to their car, Nick couldn't help but replay the day's events in his mind. He questioned himself, wondering if there was something he could have done differently.

"Nick?" Sandra's voice broke through his thoughts. "You're doing everything you can. We both are."

He squeezed her hand, grateful for her support. "I know, but I can't shake the feeling that we're running out of time."

"Hey," Sandra met his gaze, determination shining in her eyes. "We're going to find him. I promise."

They reached the car, the once welcoming interior now a reminder of their missing son. Nick pulled out his phone, his fingers tapping out the number for the Elk County Sheriff's Department with an urgency that matched his racing heart.

"Elk County Sheriff's Department, how can I help you?" the operator answered.

"Hi, my name is Nick Harris. My wife and I are at a diner off Highway 50, and our son has gone missing. We've searched everywhere and can't find any trace of him. Can you please send someone?"

"Of course, Mr. Harris. A deputy will be sent to your location as soon as possible. Please stay there and wait for their arrival."

"Thank you," Nick said, his voice barely above a whisper. He ended the call and stared at the phone screen, feeling helpless and vulnerable.

Sandra leaned against him, her body trembling with silent sobs. "We'll find him, Nick. We have to."

As they waited for the deputy to arrive, the sun dipped below the horizon, casting ominous shadows across the desolate landscape. The weight of their fear and uncertainty pressed down on them, suffocating, as they faced the unknown that lay ahead.

CHAPTER 2

Nick's heart raced as he darted between the diner tables, his eyes frantically scanning the area for any sign of Jamie. Sandra followed suit, her face flushed with panic and worry. They exchanged desperate glances, their fear mounting with each passing second.

"Jamie!" Sandra called out, her voice cracking under the strain. "Jamie, where are you?"

The diner itself was a nondescript roadside establishment, its faded paint barely clinging to the walls. The windows were smudged with dust and grime, offering little respite from the sweltering heat outside. The surroundings only served to heighten their sense of isolation, the vast desert stretching out around them like an oppressive blanket.

"Did you check the bathroom?" Nick asked, his voice tight with concern.

"Twice," Sandra replied, biting her lip. "He's not there."

"Damn it!" Nick slammed his fist onto a nearby table, causing the silverware to rattle loudly. "Where could he be? He was just here a minute ago!"

"Maybe someone saw something?" Sandra suggested, though her voice wavered with uncertainty.

"Excuse me, ma'am," Nick addressed a waitress who happened to pass by. "Have you seen our son? He's about this tall" – he held up his hand to indicate Jamie's height – "and has curly blonde hair."

"Sorry, sir," the waitress replied, shaking her head. "I haven't seen anyone that fits that description. But I'll let you know if I do."

"Thank you," Sandra said, trying to keep her composure. "We really appreciate it."

"Let's check the parking lot again," Nick proposed, his chest tightening with every labored breath. "He might've gone outside for some fresh air."

Sandra nodded, and they hurried back out into the glaring sunlight. The heat bore down on them like a physical weight, the air thick and suffocating. Nick wiped the sweat from his brow as they scanned the parking lot, their despair growing with each passing moment.

"Jamie!" Nick yelled again, hoping against hope that his son would emerge from behind one of the parked cars. "Come on, buddy! This isn't funny!"

"Nick," Sandra choked out, her hands trembling. "What if something happened to him? What if someone took him?"

"Let's not jump to conclusions," Nick tried to reassure her, though he couldn't keep the tremor from his voice. "We'll find him, Sandra. We have to."

As they continued their desperate search, both Nick and Sandra knew that time was of the essence. And in this desolate place, under the unforgiving desert sun, it seemed as if time itself was running out.

Nick's heart pounded in his ears as he and Sandra circled the parking lot, their voices growing hoarse from calling Jamie's name. The stifling heat seemed to choke them, making it difficult to breathe, but they couldn't afford to slow down.

"Jamie!" Sandra cried out, her eyes darting from one dusty car to another. "Please, answer us!"

"Maybe he went further down the road," Nick suggested, trying to keep his voice steady. "Or into the desert for some reason."

"Into the desert?" Sandra's face paled at the thought. "No, no, he wouldn't do that. He knows better."

"Alright, let's think," said Nick, stopping for a moment to catch his breath. "Where else could he have gone?"

As they stood there, lost in thought, a shadow fell over them. They looked up to see Sheriff Daniel Wallace approaching, his stern expression and graying hair giving him an air of authority.

"Is there a problem here?" the sheriff asked, his deep voice laced with impatience.

"Our son is missing," Nick blurted out, desperation clear in his tone. "We were just inside the diner, and when we came back out, he was gone."

"Missing?" Sheriff Wallace raised an eyebrow skeptically. "How long has he been gone?"

"About twenty minutes," Sandra answered, trying to maintain eye contact with the sheriff, whose gaze seemed to bore right through her.

"Probably just wandered off somewhere," the sheriff dismissed, waving a hand nonchalantly. "Kids do that all the time."

"Excuse me, but our son isn't like that," Nick interjected, frustration simmering beneath his words. "He knows better than to wander off without telling us."

"Besides," Sandra added, her voice shaking with anger, "this area isn't exactly safe. We're in the middle of a desert, and it's scorching hot. Anything could happen."

"Look," Sheriff Wallace sighed, clearly annoyed. "I'll keep an eye out for him. But I suggest you two keep looking as well. He couldn't have gone far."

As the sheriff walked away, leaving Nick and Sandra to their own devices, they both knew they couldn't rely on him for help.

"Come on," Nick said, his jaw clenched with determination. "We're going to find Jamie ourselves."

Nick's heart pounded in his chest, his eyes darting from one corner of the parking lot to the other. Sandra's gaze mirrored his own as they searched desperately for any sign of their son.

"Please, Sheriff," Sandra pleaded, her voice cracking with fear. "You have to help us find Jamie. He's just a kid, and he could be in danger."

"Listen," Nick chimed in, trying to keep his voice steady despite the panic gnawing at him. "We've never had anything like this happen before. We're really worried about our boy."

"Alright, alright," Sheriff Wallace sighed, holding up a hand to silence them. "As I said earlier, kids wander off all the time. It's nothing to get worked up over."

"Please don't take this lightly," Sandra begged, tears brimming in her eyes. "We need your help."

"Fine," the sheriff relented, but his tone remained dismissive. "I'll call it in, have some deputies look around. But I'm telling you, he probably just found something that caught his eye and got sidetracked."

Nick exchanged a glance with Sandra, both sharing the same sinking feeling that the sheriff wasn't taking their concerns seriously. Still, they couldn't afford to waste any more time arguing with him. Every second mattered in finding Jamie.

"Thank you," Nick managed to say, barely concealing his frustration. "We'll keep looking too. If you hear anything—"

"Of course," Sheriff Wallace interrupted, already turning away from them. "I'll let you know."

As he walked off, Nick clenched his fists, struggling to contain his anger. Sandra wiped away a tear, her face etched with worry. They knew they were on their own, and that only fueled their determination to find Jamie.

"Let's check behind the diner," Nick suggested, his voice low and tense. "Maybe he went exploring."

"Okay," Sandra agreed, nodding. "We'll find him, Nick. We have to."

Together, they headed toward the back of the diner, their steps hurried. Though they tried to stay hopeful, the weight of their son's disappearance and the sheriff's indifference hung heavily over them like a dark cloud, threatening to suffocate their resolve.

Nick's eyes narrowed as he watched Sheriff Wallace saunter away, his heart pounding with a mix of frustration and fear. Sandra's hand clenched around his arm, her knuckles white, her voice trembling with barely contained fury.

"Is that it?" she demanded, turning back to the sheriff. "You're just going to call it in and hope for the best? Our son is missing, damn it!"

Sheriff Wallace paused, and with an exasperated sigh, turned back to face them. "Mrs. Harris, I understand you're upset—"

"Upset?" Nick cut him off, incredulous. "Our child is out there, alone, and you don't seem to give a damn!"

"Watch your tone," the sheriff warned, his expression hardening. "I'm doing my job."

"Your job?" Sandra scoffed. "You haven't even looked around! You're not taking this seriously at all!"

"Listen," Sheriff Wallace said, annoyance creeping into his voice. "This is a small town. Kids wander off all the time. They always come back, so let's just give it some time before we start panicking, alright?"

"Every minute matters!" Nick argued, his voice strained. "We need you to act now, not later! What if he's hurt or—" He couldn't bring himself to say it, the thought too unbearable to entertain.

"Alright, alright," the sheriff relented, raising his hands in mock surrender. "I'll have my men do a thorough search of the area. Satisfied?"

"Hardly," Sandra snapped, her eyes burning with anger. "But it's better than nothing."

"Trust me, folks," Sheriff Wallace said, his voice dripping with condescension. "Your boy will turn up safe and sound. Just try to stay calm and let us handle it."

As the sheriff walked away, his disinterest leaving a bitter taste in their mouths, Nick and Sandra shared a look of mutual disgust.

"He's not going to help us," Sandra whispered, her voice shaking with a mix of fear and anger. "We'll have to find Jamie ourselves."

"Damn right we will," Nick agreed, gritting his teeth. "No one is going to stop us from finding our son."

Nick clenched his fists, watching as Sheriff Wallace sauntered away without a care in the world. He could feel Sandra's gaze on him, her fear and frustration mirroring his own.

"Can you believe this?" Nick muttered, shaking his head in disbelief. "He doesn't give a damn about Jamie."

"Who the hell does he think he is?" Sandra seethed, her eyes flashing with anger. "We can't trust him to find our son. We have to do something, Nick."

"Alright, let's start by rechecking the diner," Nick suggested, determination filling his voice. "We'll talk to everyone we can, see if anyone saw anything."

"Good idea," Sandra agreed, her voice wavering slightly. "And we'll keep calling Jamie's name. Maybe he'll hear us and come back."

As they made their way back into the diner, Nick couldn't help but notice how empty it felt now. The few patrons who had been there earlier seemed to have disappeared, leaving them alone with their desperation.

"Excuse me," Nick said, approaching the waitress who had served them earlier. "Did you see our son leave? Did anyone come in after us?"

The waitress shook her head, her expression full of sympathy. "I'm sorry, I didn't see anything. But I'll keep an eye out for him, I promise."

"Thank you," Sandra whispered, gratitude shining in her eyes despite the tears threatening to spill over.

"Let's go check outside again," Nick urged, grabbing Sandra's hand and leading her back into the sweltering heat.

The door of the diner slammed shut behind them, a sudden gust of hot air whipping across their faces as they stepped back into the unforgiving desert. Nick and Sandra exchanged glances, both sets of eyes filled with determination, but also uncertainty about where to turn next.

"Listen," Nick said, his voice low and steady. "We can't rely on that sheriff. We're going to have to find Jamie ourselves."

Sandra nodded, her hands trembling at her sides. "But where do we even start? This place is so isolated, he could be anywhere."

"Let's start with the area around the diner," Nick suggested. "Maybe there are tracks or something we missed in our panic."

"Right," Sandra agreed, taking a deep breath to steady herself. "We'll just...we'll have to look harder. We'll find him, Nick. We have to."

Together, they began scanning the ground, searching for any clue that might lead them to their son. The sun beat down upon them mercilessly, sweat dripping from their brows as they combed through the sand and rocks surrounding the parking lot.

"Nick, over here!" Sandra called out suddenly, her voice filled with urgency. She pointed to a set of footprints in the sand where their car was parked leading away. "These look fresh. They could be Jamie's."

"Good eye," Nick said, relief momentarily flashing across his face. "Let's follow them, see where they lead."

As they traced the path of the footprints, Nick couldn't shake the growing sense of unease that gnawed at his gut. "Sandra, why would Jamie have wandered off like this? It doesn't make sense."

"I don't know," Sandra admitted, her voice cracking. "I just hope he's alright."

"Hey," Nick said softly, reaching out to touch her arm. "We're going to find him, okay? We won't stop until we do."

"Okay," Sandra whispered, her eyes filled with a mixture of gratitude and fear. "Thank you, Nick."

"Let's keep moving," Nick urged, his voice firm but gentle. "We've got a lot of ground to cover."

As they pressed on through the sweltering heat, following the trail left by the mysterious footprints, the weight of their mission seemed to grow heavier with each passing moment. The vast expanse of desert stretched out before them, seemingly endless and unforgiving.

But neither Nick nor Sandra wavered in their resolve. They were determined to find their son, no matter what it took – even if it meant facing the unknown dangers that lurked just beyond the horizon.

CHAPTER 3

Detective Rachel Valdez pushed open the heavy glass doors of the Elk County Sheriff's Department, her sharp brown eyes immediately scanning the room for Sheriff Daniel Wallace. The scent of stale coffee and the faint humming of fluorescent lights filled the air. She adjusted the strap of her leather shoulder bag, feeling the weight of responsibility settling on her as she took a step forward.

Rachel's gaze narrowed as she watched the receptionist lazily chew her gum, seemingly unbothered by the mention of the missing boy. The woman's lack of urgency irked Valdez; it was as if she couldn't care less about a potentially life-threatening situation. Rachel clenched her fist momentarily, trying to remind herself that not everyone shared her sense of responsibility and commitment.

"Sure thing, Detective," drawled the receptionist as she picked up the phone. "I'll let Sheriff Wallace know you're here." Before she had even finished dialing, the office door swung open, revealing the imposing figure of Sheriff Daniel Wallace.

"Detective Valdez?" he boomed, his graying hair slicked back and his stern expression giving him an air of authority that demanded respect. Valdez turned towards him, noting how his demeanor contrasted starkly with the receptionist's nonchalance.

"Sheriff Wallace," she said, nodding her head in acknowledgement. "I'm here regarding the Harris family's missing son."

"Ah, yes." He scanned the room before gesturing for her to follow him into his office. As they walked, Valdez couldn't help but feel a growing sense of skepticism. She wondered if the sheriff shared the same indifference towards Jamie's disappearance as his receptionist, or if his stoic facade hid something far more sinister.

"Please, have a seat," Sheriff Wallace offered once they were inside his office. Rachel sat down, her eyes never leaving his face.

"Thank you, Sheriff," she replied, maintaining her composure. "I've been looking into similar cases recently, and I can't help but feel there's more to this than meets the eye."

"Such as?" He raised an eyebrow, leaning back in his chair.

"Two other boys have gone missing in the past six months, all within a hundred-mile radius. And yet, no solid leads or connections have been found," Valdez explained.

"Coincidence," the sheriff replied dismissively. "These things happen sometimes."

"Maybe," Valdez conceded, though she didn't believe it for a second. "But I'd like to take a closer look at the case files and any evidence collected so far."

Sheriff Wallace hesitated before finally nodding. "Alright, detective. I'll have someone gather the files for you."

Rachel Valdez stared at the framed picture on Sheriff Wallace's desk, a family photo with him and his wife proudly holding their two young children. She wondered if he had ever genuinely cared about other people or if it was all just an act.

"Is there something you wanted to say, Detective?" Sheriff Wallace asked, breaking her out of her thoughts.

"Actually, yes," she replied, meeting his gaze once more. "I'm concerned about the way this case has been handled so far. Why hasn't there been a more thorough search for Jamie Harris? This is a small town; surely his disappearance should be a top priority."

"Detective Valdez," Sheriff Wallace sighed, clearly annoyed by her persistence, "I understand your concern, but we have limited resources here. We've done what we can, and the search continues."

"Does it, though?" Rachel shot back, unable to hide the disbelief in her voice. "It seems like everyone around here is treating Jamie's disappearance as just another trivial matter. A teen goes missing, and life goes on as usual?"

"Detective, Elk County isn't immune to crime," Wallace replied, leaning forward and resting his elbows on his desk. "We've had our fair share of cases over the years, and we do our best to handle them all. I assure you, we're doing everything we can for Jamie."

"Two other boys have gone missing in the past six months," Valdez countered, her eyes narrowing. "All within a hundred-mile radius. Does that not worry you, Sheriff?"

"Of course it does," he said, his tone dripping with condescension. "But we can't jump to conclusions without any solid evidence. As far as we know, these boys could have run away from home or gotten lost on their own accord."

"Or they could be victims of something much worse," Valdez insisted, her gut telling her this wasn't a coincidence. "I'm not trying to accuse you or your department of negligence, Sheriff, but the facts speak for themselves. I strongly believe there's more to this case than what we've been led to believe."

"Your point is noted, Detective," Wallace said dismissively, leaning back in his chair and crossing his arms. "But until there's concrete evidence to support your theory, I suggest we stick to the facts we have and continue our search for Jamie."

Valdez clenched her jaw, frustration bubbling beneath the surface. She knew she couldn't force the sheriff to take her suspicions seriously, but she was determined to uncover the truth, no matter how hard he tried to downplay the situation.

Frustration clouded Valdez's vision as she took a deep breath, focusing on the facts laid out before her. She locked eyes with Sheriff Wallace, steeling herself for the challenge she was about to present.

"Let me remind you, Sheriff," Valdez began, her voice steady but firm, "that each of these boys disappeared under similar circumstances – all were last seen alone, near wooded areas, and no trace of them has been found since."

Sheriff Wallace raised an eyebrow but said nothing, his expression unreadable.

"Furthermore," Valdez continued, "despite the similarities in their cases, there seems to have been little effort made to connect them. No task force has been established, no public warnings issued. It's almost as if these disappearances are being intentionally kept separate."

Wallace scoffed. "That's quite an accusation, Detective. But I assure you, we've considered every angle in these investigations."

"Then why haven't you shared this information with other departments, or reached out to experts who might be able to help?" Valdez pressed, feeling her determination grow. "I'm not accusing anyone of wrongdoing, Sheriff, but there's clearly something missing here."

"Detective Valdez," Wallace replied coolly, "we run our department as we see fit. You may not agree with our methods, but our priority is finding these boys and bringing them home safely."

"Then let me help," Valdez insisted, leaning forward in her seat. "Give me access to the case files and any evidence collected so far. If there's nothing to hide, there should be no issue with me taking a closer look."

The silence that followed felt heavy, as Valdez held her breath, waiting for Wallace's response. She knew she was taking a risk by pushing him, but the thought of these boys, potentially in danger, propelled her forward. She could not, and would not, back down.

Sheriff Wallace's eyes narrowed, a bead of sweat forming at his temple. He looked Valdez up and down, weighing his options, before finally releasing a reluctant sigh. "Fine," he said tersely. "I'll grant you access to the case files."

"Thank you, Sheriff," Valdez replied, keeping her tone neutral, though inside she was brimming with anticipation. This was her chance to dig deeper, to find what had been overlooked or intentionally obscured.

"Follow me," Wallace commanded, leading her through the narrow halls of the sheriff's department. The walls seemed to close in around them as they made their way towards the evidence room, and Valdez felt a shiver run down her spine.

Upon entering the room, Valdez's eyes immediately darted to the shelves lined with boxes and bags of evidence. She could feel her pulse quicken, knowing that somewhere among these items lay the clues she needed to uncover the truth.

"Here are the case files," Wallace grunted, handing her a thick stack of folders. "Everything else is in those cabinets." He gestured with a nod of his head, his expression unreadable.

"Much appreciated," Valdez replied, her focus already on the folders in her hands. She took a seat at a nearby table, spreading the files out before her. Each one represented a missing boy, a family left with a gaping hole, waiting for answers.

"Remember, Detective," Wallace warned, his voice low and menacing. "You're a guest here. Don't overstep your boundaries."

Valdez glanced up briefly, meeting his gaze. "I'm just here to help, Sheriff," she responded evenly, her eyes locking onto his for a moment before she turned her attention back to the files.

As Valdez began leafing through the documents, her curiosity piqued. She noticed patterns emerging – similarities between the boys and their disappearances that couldn't be mere coincidence. The victims were all around the same age, and each had vanished without a trace.

"Could these be connected?" Valdez murmured to herself, her thoughts racing. "Is there something tying them together?"

Her mind swam with questions, her intuition telling her that the answers lay within these pages. She just needed to sift through the information, to piece together the puzzle that had eluded the sheriff's department for so long. And she was determined to do just that – no matter what obstacles stood in her way.

Valdez's fingers traced the edges of a photograph, her eyes narrowing as she studied the image. It was a group shot from a recent community event – Sheriff Wallace standing front and center, surrounded by smiling townsfolk. But it was the subtle, almost imperceptible shift in his posture when positioned near the missing boys that caught her attention.

"Something doesn't add up," Valdez muttered under her breath.

Detective Valdez sat at the small table, her fingers tapping rhythmically against the case files. Her eyes narrowed as she pieced together the fragments of information she had collected. Each new detail seemed to only deepen the mystery surrounding Jamie's disappearance, while simultaneously raising more questions about Sheriff Wallace's involvement.

"Detective, I've been thinking about what you asked me earlier," Nick said, breaking the silence that had settled over the room. "About anything unusual happening before Jamie went missing."

"Go on," Valdez urged, leaning in closer to hear him.

"Jamie mentioned a man hanging around his school a few days before he disappeared. He said the guy was creepy and kept watching the kids. I dismissed it at the time, thinking it was just some drifter passing through town. But now..." Nick's voice trailed off as though he were afraid to say any more.

"Did you tell Sheriff Wallace about this?" Valdez asked, her pulse quickening with every word.

"No, it never crossed my mind to mention it. Like I said, I didn't think it was important at the time," Nick admitted, shame coloring his face.

"Can you describe the man Jamie saw?" Valdez pressed, knowing that every detail could be crucial.

"Jamie said he was tall and thin, with dark hair. But other than that, I don't have much to go on," Nick replied, clearly frustrated by the lack of information.

Valdez frowned, mulling over the revelation. It wasn't much, but it was a lead – something she could work with. As she considered the information, the lingering skepticism she'd felt towards the investigation began to ebb, replaced by a growing sense of urgency. She couldn't shake the feeling that Jamie was in danger, and that time was running out.

"Mr. Harris, I want you to know that I'm taking your son's case very seriously," Valdez said, her voice firm and resolute. "I won't rest until we've found Jamie and brought him back home safely."

"Thank you, Detective. That means more to us than you can imagine," Nick replied, his eyes glistening with unshed tears.

"Rest assured, Mr. Harris, I'll do everything in my power to uncover the truth behind these disappearances," Valdez vowed, her determination unwavering.

As she watched Nick walk away, Valdez's fingers curled around the edge of the case files, her resolve hardening into steel. She knew that she was about to embark on a treacherous path – one that would test her skills, her instincts, and her commitment to justice. But if it meant finding Jamie and putting an end to this nightmare, Valdez was ready to face whatever challenges lay ahead.

Nick's voice echoed in Valdez's head, reminding her of the urgency at hand. She glanced down at the case files spread across the table, a strategy already taking shape in her mind. Sandra Harris stood by her husband, her eyes filled with a mix of gratitude and fear.

"Alright," Valdez began, her tone decisive. "Here's what we're going to do."

She looked between Nick and Sandra, making sure she had their full attention. "We'll start by searching the area where the car was parked. We need to find – anything – that could help us piece together his movements."

"Of course," Sandra agreed, her voice tight with determination. "We've already spoken with some of the neighbors, but we'll go back and ask again."

"Good," Valdez nodded. "While you two are doing that, I'll be following up on a few leads from these case files. There are certain inconsistencies I want to get to the bottom of before we proceed with the investigation."

"Detective Valdez," Nick interjected, his hands clasping together anxiously. "I know you don't want us to get our hopes up, but... Do you really think there's a chance we'll find him?"

Valdez hesitated for a moment, weighing her words carefully. She didn't want to give false hope, but she also understood the importance of maintaining their resolve. "I can't make any promises, Mr. Harris," she admitted. "But I can tell you this: I've seen cases with fewer leads and worse odds come through with positive outcomes. We have to stay focused and work methodically if we want to bring Jamie home."

"Thank you, Detective," Sandra murmured, her grip tightening around Nick's hand.

"Time is of the essence," Valdez continued, her mind racing with possibilities as she scanned the case files one more time. "We'll need to coordinate our efforts and keep each other updated on any new developments. With a solid plan in place and all of us working together, I believe we have a fighting chance."

"Let's do this," Nick said, his voice resolute, echoing Valdez's earlier determination.

Valdez nodded, mentally preparing herself for the obstacles that lay ahead. There were no guarantees in this line of work, but she would be damned if she didn't give it her all. For Jamie's sake – and for the Harris family – she had to believe they could solve this puzzle and bring him back safely.

"Alright, let's get started," she said with finality, closing the case files and tucking them under her arm. "We've got a long road ahead of us, but I'm confident that, together, we can find Jamie and uncover the truth behind these disappearances."

CHAPTER 4

The sun was setting in the distance, casting an orange glow over the desolate landscape. Nick Harris gripped the steering wheel tighter, his knuckles turning white. The car sputtered and choked before coming to a halt just outside of Elk County.

"Dammit," he muttered under his breath. Sandra looked at him, concern etched across her face.

"Nick, what's happening?" she asked, her brown eyes wide with fear.

"Car's dead," he replied tersely, feeling the weight of their situation sinking in.

"Great. Just great," Sandra sighed, rubbing her temples. "We're in the middle of nowhere, and Jamie is still missing."

"Stay calm, Sandra. We'll figure this out," Nick reassured her as he stepped out of the car and popped the hood. He stared at the engine, hoping for some kind of miraculous revelation, but nothing came.

"Need some help there, buddy?" a gruff voice called from behind him. Nick turned to see an older man approaching, his hands stained with grease. He had a rough, weathered face that spoke of hard work and determination. His eyes held a mixture of curiosity and caution.

"Uh, yeah," Nick stammered, taken aback by the sudden appearance of the stranger. "Our car just died on us."

"Name's Eddie Ramirez," the man said, extending a hand towards Nick. "I'm a mechanic around these parts. Let me take a look."

"Thanks, Eddie," Nick replied, shaking his hand firmly. "I'm Nick, and that's my wife, Sandra. We're trying to find our son, Jamie."

Eddie nodded, his expression serious. "Well, let's get this car running first. Then we can talk about your boy."

Sandra stepped out of the car, watching as Eddie expertly inspected the engine. She glanced at Nick, her eyes clouded with worry. He tried to offer her a reassuring smile but knew it fell flat.

"Alright," Eddie said after a few minutes, wiping his hands on a rag he pulled from his back pocket. "I think I know what's wrong. It's not a permanent fix, but it'll get you moving again."

"Thank you, Eddie," Sandra said, her voice trembling slightly. "We really appreciate it."

"Sure thing," Eddie replied gruffly, his no-nonsense attitude shining through. "Now let's talk about your boy."

Nick hesitated for a moment before delving into the story of Jamie's disappearance. "We think our son might have run into trouble with Sheriff Wallace," he said, keeping his voice low to avoid attracting unwanted attention.

"Wallace, huh?" Eddie grunted, narrowing his eyes. "Can't say I'm surprised. That man's got a way of making people disappear."

Sandra looked alarmed at Eddie's comment. "What do you mean? Do you know something about Jamie?"

"Easy now," Eddie replied, raising a hand in a calming gesture. "I don't know anything about your boy specifically. But I've seen enough of that damn sheriff to know he's bad news."

"Tell us more, please," Nick urged, his desperation palpable. He and Sandra exchanged glances, sensing that Eddie's words carried significant weight.

"Fine," Eddie conceded, leaning against the hood of the car. "You want my story? I'll give it to you straight."

He paused, rubbing the stubble on his chin as if considering where to begin. "My family's been in Elk County for generations. My daddy was a mechanic, just like me. But when I was a boy, this place wasn't so bad. Sure, there were some crooks and troublemakers, but nothing like what we've got now."

"Then Wallace came along," Eddie continued, his voice growing darker. "He started out as a deputy, but he quickly climbed the ranks. Next thing you know, he's sheriff. And that's when things really went south."

"Are you saying he's corrupt?" Sandra asked cautiously, her brown eyes searching Eddie's face for answers.

"Corrupt doesn't even begin to cover it," Eddie replied bitterly. "That man is pure evil. He's got a taste for power and control, and he uses his badge as an excuse to hurt people. I've seen it with my own eyes."

"Is that why you hate him?" Nick asked, attempting to understand the depth of Eddie's vendetta against Sheriff Wallace.

"Part of it," Eddie admitted, his gaze distant as he recalled painful memories. "The main reason is personal. My baby sister went missing years ago, and I'm convinced Wallace had something to do with it. But nobody would listen to me. They all thought I was crazy."

"Jesus," Sandra whispered, her hand covering her mouth in shock. "I'm so sorry, Eddie."

"Don't be," Eddie said gruffly, waving off her sympathy. "It ain't your fault. But if there's even a chance that I can help you find your boy and make that son of a bitch pay, then count me in."

"Thank you," Nick replied, his voice thick with gratitude. "We appreciate your help more than we can say."

"Let's just hope we can find Jamie before it's too late," Eddie muttered ominously, casting a wary glance down the desolate road that lay ahead.

Eddie squatted down beside the Harris family's broken-down car, his eyes narrowed as he inspected the underbelly. Nick and Sandra hovered nearby, their gazes following Eddie's every move.

"Looks like your fuel pump's shot," Eddie muttered, his fingers tracing over the damaged part. "It's no wonder you couldn't get anywhere."

"Is there any way to fix it?" Nick asked, a flicker of hope in his voice.

"Out here? Not gonna be easy," Eddie admitted, running a hand through his greying hair. "But I might have a workaround that'll get you back on the road for now. Just don't expect it to last forever."

"Anything helps," Sandra replied gratefully. "We need to keep searching for our son."

"Understood," Eddie said with a curt nod. He rummaged through his toolbox, producing a roll of duct tape and a few other makeshift supplies. As he worked, his knowledgeable hands moved with precision and confidence, showcasing his years of experience as a mechanic in Elk County.

"Y'know, this isn't my first time dealing with car troubles out in the desert," Eddie shared, glancing at Nick and Sandra. "I've seen all kinds of breakdowns and accidents out here. It's not an easy place to navigate, especially if you're not familiar with the terrain."

"Which is why we're lucky to have found you," Nick said, his tone sincere. "Your expertise could make all the difference in finding Jamie."

"Damn right," Eddie grunted, securing the final piece of duct tape. "This should hold up for a while, but I'd recommend getting it properly fixed once you're back in town."

"Thank you, Eddie," Sandra said, her eyes shining with gratitude. "You're giving us a fighting chance to find our boy and bring Sheriff Wallace to justice."

"Like I said, count me in," Eddie replied, determination etched onto his weathered face. "We'll find your son, and we'll make sure that bastard pays for what he's done."

Nick and Sandra exchanged glances, their resolve strengthened by Eddie's unwavering commitment. Together, they were one step closer to finding Jamie and exposing the corruption that had plagued their lives.

"Let's do this," Nick murmured, clapping a hand on Eddie's shoulder. "For Jamie."

"For Jamie," Eddie agreed, his voice steeling with resolve as they prepared to face the challenges ahead.

With the car now running, albeit temporarily, Eddie wiped his greasy hands on a rag and turned to face Nick and Sandra. The late afternoon sun cast long shadows across the desert landscape, highlighting the determination that radiated from the trio.

"Alright, we're in this together," Eddie said, his gruff voice filled with resolve. "Now, I've got an idea of where we should start lookin'. Wallace has a few spots he likes to frequent when he ain't on duty. We might be able to dig up some information there."

"Sounds like a plan," Nick agreed, nodding at Eddie's suggestion.

"Where exactly are these places?" Sandra asked, her brow furrowed in worry but ready to face whatever might come their way.

"There's a bar called The Rusty Spur – it's just outside town," Eddie replied, scratching at his stubble as he thought. "And there's an old warehouse near the train tracks where Wallace sometimes goes to 'conduct business,' if you catch my drift."

"Right," Nick muttered, understanding the implication. "We'll have to approach both places carefully. We don't want to alert Wallace or any of his cronies that we're onto him."

"Agreed," Eddie said, his eyes narrowing as he considered their options. "I know a couple of folks around here who might be willing to talk – people who've had run-ins with Wallace before and ain't too pleased with how he runs things."

"Good," Sandra murmured, her heart pounding in her chest. "The more people we can get on our side, the better our chances of finding Jamie and putting an end to Wallace's reign of terror."

"Before we head out, though," Eddie added, his voice cautious, "we gotta make sure we're prepared for anything. If things go south, we need to be able to protect ourselves – and each other."

"Of course," Nick replied, his hand instinctively going to the small pocketknife he kept in his jacket. "We'll do whatever it takes to keep our family safe and bring Jamie home."

"Then let's get moving," Eddie said, his eyes meeting those of his newfound allies. "Every minute counts."

As they climbed into their car, Nick couldn't help but feel a renewed sense of hope and determination. Together with Eddie, they would face whatever challenges lay ahead, and they wouldn't rest until Jamie was safely back in their arms.

The sun dipped below the horizon, casting eerie shadows across the desert landscape as Eddie unfolded a dusty map and spread it out on the hood of the car. Nick and Sandra leaned in, their eyes scanning the worn paper for clues to Jamie's whereabouts.

"Here," Eddie said, pointing to a cluster of markings. "These are places where Wallace has been known to hang around – bars, diners, that sort of thing. If we're gonna get any leads on Jamie, these are the places we should start."

"Alright," Nick said, his fingers tracing the winding roads. "We'll split up and cover more ground. Sandra, you take the east side and I'll head west."

"Sounds like a plan," Sandra agreed, trying to memorize the locations Eddie pointed out. "What about navigating through this terrain, though? We're not exactly local experts."

Eddie chuckled, his gruff voice filled with hard-earned knowledge. "Don't worry, I got that covered too. When it comes to the desert, I know every inch of this place like the back of my hand. Just remember, always keep an eye on the landmarks – they'll help guide you through the vastness."

"Thanks, Eddie," Sandra said, her gratitude genuine. "Your expertise will be invaluable in our search."

"Speaking of which," Nick interjected, his brow furrowed in concern, "why are you so committed to helping us, Eddie? Not that we don't appreciate it, but you barely know us."

Eddie sighed, his gaze dropping to the map. "I've had my own run-ins with Sheriff Wallace," he admitted, his voice tinged with bitterness. "He's a sadistic bastard who takes pleasure in causing pain to others – and he ain't above using his authority to do it. I've seen firsthand how his twisted mind works, and trust me, you don't want to be on his bad side."

"God, that's awful," Sandra whispered, her heart aching for the pain Eddie must have endured. "We can't let him continue to terrorize this community."

"Exactly," Eddie replied, his eyes steeling with determination. "That's why I'm in this fight with you, until the very end. We're gonna bring that sick son of a bitch down and make sure he never hurts anyone again – Jamie or otherwise."

"Thank you, Eddie," Nick said, clapping the mechanic on the shoulder. "Together, we'll put an end to Wallace's reign of terror and bring our boy home."

As the trio prepared to embark on their separate missions, they exchanged a look of shared resolve. United by their common goal, they would face the dangers of the desert and the sinister machinations of Sheriff Wallace – and they would not rest until justice was served.

Eddie traced a finger along the map, stopping on a small, unmarked area nestled between rocky hills. "I've got a place we can use as a base of operations," he said, his voice low and steady. "It's an old cabin I know about – off the grid, hardly anyone knows it exists. We can meet there to regroup and share what we find."

"Sounds perfect," Nick replied, studying the map intently. He could feel the weight of responsibility bearing down on him, but with Eddie's knowledge and expertise, their chances of finding Jamie seemed more hopeful.

"Thank you so much, Eddie," Sandra said, her eyes brimming with gratitude. "We can't tell you how much your help means to us."

"Hey, don't mention it," Eddie responded gruffly, his cheeks reddening slightly. "You're good people, and I couldn't just stand by and do nothing."

Nick looked around at the desolate landscape, feeling the seconds ticking by like hours. "We should get moving," he suggested. "The sooner we start, the better chance we have of finding Jamie before Wallace can cover his tracks."

"Agreed," Eddie nodded, folding up the map and handing it to Nick. "Remember, keep your eyes open and be ready for anything. This desert can be unforgiving, and so can the people who live here."

"Got it," Sandra confirmed, her jaw set in determination. She locked eyes with Eddie, conveying her resolve without words. Together, they would navigate the treacherous terrain and confront the evil lurking in the shadows.

"Good luck, you two," Eddie said as he turned to leave. "I'll see you at the cabin. And remember, stay safe out there."

"Thank you, Eddie. See you soon," Nick called after him, then turned to his wife. "Let's do this, Sandra. Let's find our son."

With renewed determination, Nick and Sandra set off driving into the desert, following the map provided by their newfound ally. The path ahead was fraught with danger and uncertainty, but they would face it head-on, united in their pursuit of justice – and the truth about Jamie's disappearance.

CHAPTER 5

The dim light from the motel room's solitary lamp cast eerie shadows on the faces of Valdez and the Harris family as they huddled around the small table, a jumble of papers and photographs spread before them. The air was thick with tension; each person intently focused on the task at hand – finding Jamie.

"Alright," Valdez began, rubbing her temples, "let's go over our leads again." She picked up a file and flipped it open, scanning its contents. Nick clenched his fists, his face a mask of determination. Sandra looked at him; concern etched on her features.

"Detective, we have to find him soon. Who knows what that monster is doing to him?" Nick's voice trembled with desperation. Valdez met his gaze, her brown eyes filled with quiet resolve.

"Mr. Harris, I assure you, we're doing everything in our power to find your son." Her eyes flicked back to the file, and she paused for a moment, a frown creasing her forehead. The Sheriff had found two boys dead, but no further action was taken. Their parents hadn't even been notified? Valdez felt a cold knot of anger form in her stomach, but she couldn't let this information distract her – not now, not when they were so close to finding Jamie. She made a mental note to revisit this issue later and kept the discovery to herself.

"Maybe we should focus on the areas where the other missing boys were found," Sandra suggested, her voice steady and rational. "There might be some clues there."

"Good idea, Mrs. Harris," Valdez agreed, impressed by the woman's composure. "Let's see..." She trailed off, studying the map and tracing her finger along the various locations marked on it.

"Every second counts, Detective," Nick interjected, frustration seeping into his words. "We can't afford to waste any more time."

"Mr. Harris, I understand, but we have to be thorough," Valdez replied, her tone firm yet compassionate. "We don't want to overlook anything that might lead us to Jamie."

"I know," Nick sighed, his eyes glistening with unshed tears. "I just...I can't bear the thought of him out there, scared and alone."

Valdez reached across the table and placed a hand on his arm, offering a reassuring squeeze. "We're going to find him, Mr. Harris. I promise you that. Together, we'll bring him home."

Nick paced back and forth, his shoes scuffing against the worn motel carpet as Sandra sat on the edge of the bed. Valdez looked up from the map, her eyes narrowing in thought. "You know, there's a lot of desert around that diner where Jamie went missing," she said slowly. "And it's not far from some of the areas where those other boys were first seen."

"Are you suggesting we go out there and search?" Nick asked his voice tight with desperation.

"Exactly," Valdez replied, her determination evident. "I think there might be clues or patterns in that area that could give us potential evidence leading to Jamie."

"Then what are we waiting for?" Sandra stood, her face set with resolve. "Let's get moving."

Valdez nodded and began making a list of necessary supplies. "We'll need water, flashlights, a map of the desert...anything else you can think of that might be useful."

As the Harrises frantically gathered supplies, Valdez slipped out the door to make a call. Her voice was hushed as she spoke into the phone, requesting any help or intel they could provide on the case. She knew their first plan was to search the desolate desert and abandoned structures near the diner, hoping for any clues that could lead them to Jamie. But deep down, Valdez felt conflicted – part of her wanted to uncover the truth, while another part feared what they might discover.

"Understood, Detective," came the reply. "We'll send over what we have right away."

"Thanks," Valdez said before hanging up. She returned to the room and found the family packing their supplies, each of them focused on the task at hand. Valdez couldn't help but admire their strength and determination.

"Alright," she announced, surveying their progress. "Once we have everything, we'll head out. Stay sharp, and remember – our priority is finding Jamie."

They shared resolute nods, each lost in their thoughts as they prepared for the difficult journey ahead. Every second that ticked by felt like an eternity, and they knew that with each passing moment, Jamie's chances of being found alive grew slimmer. But they refused to give up hope, refusing to let fear and despair overtake them. Together, they would search the unforgiving desert, driven by love, determination, and the unwavering belief that they would bring Jamie home.

The sun bore down on Valdez and the Harris family as they stepped out of their motel room, the heat suffocating them like a heavy blanket. Squinting against the blinding light, Nick shielded his eyes with one hand while gripping a water bottle in the other.

"Ready?" Valdez asked, her voice steady despite the oppressive heat.

"Let's find our boy," Nick said, determination etched on his face.

"Agreed," Sandra chimed in, adjusting her hat to keep the sun off her face.

As the group began their trek into the vast desert, an eerie silence enveloped them, broken only by the crunching sound of their footsteps on the dry, cracked earth. Valdez led the way, her keen eyes scanning the expanse for any possible signs of Jamie or clues that could point them in the right direction.

"Hey, Valdez," Nick called out after a while, his voice hoarse from the dry air. "You think there might be some abandoned buildings around here? Maybe Jamie sought shelter in one of them."

"Good idea, Nick," Valdez replied, nodding in approval. "Keep an eye out for anything that looks like it could've been used as a hideout."

"Will do," he responded, a glimmer of hope flickering in his eyes.

Sandra walked alongside Valdez, her maternal instincts urging her to press on despite the physical strain. *Jamie, if you're out there*, she thought, *we're coming for you.*

"Look!" Valdez suddenly exclaimed, pointing toward a dilapidated shack barely visible in the distance. "That might be worth checking out."

"Let's go," Sandra urged, picking up her pace.

The group hurried over to the structure, its weather-beaten exterior offering little protection from the elements. They approached cautiously, hearts pounding in anticipation.

"Be careful," Valdez warned as they entered, the scent of dust and decay filling their nostrils. "There might still be someone here."

"Jamie?" Sandra whispered, her voice trembling with hope and fear.

"Or whoever took him," Nick added grimly, his protective instincts on high alert.

They searched the shack thoroughly, sifting through debris and overturned furniture, desperate for any trace of Jamie. Though no immediate signs were found, Valdez discovered something that caught her attention.

"Guys," she called out, holding up a torn piece of fabric. "This could be from Jamie's shirt. We need to keep looking."

"Are you sure?" Sandra asked, desperation clear in her voice.

"Can't say for certain," Valdez admitted, her brown eyes focused on the cloth. "But it's the closest lead we've got. And if there's even a chance that Jamie was here, we can't afford to waste it."

"Right," Nick agreed, his resolve strengthening. "Let's keep searching."

As they continued to comb through the desert, their determination unwavering, Valdez couldn't help but feel a sense of responsibility for the Harris family. She knew the odds were against them, but she refused to let that shake her belief in their mission. *We will find Jamie*, she vowed silently. *No matter what it takes.*

Sweat dripped from Valdez's forehead as she spotted the small, hidden cave amidst the rocky outcrop. "Over there," she said, pointing it out to Nick and Sandra. "Could be worth checking out."

"Jamie might be in there?" Sandra asked, her voice a mixture of hope and anxiety.

"Maybe," Valdez replied, narrowing her eyes at the cave entrance. "Or whoever took him."

"Let's go then," Nick said, determination lacing his tone.

As they approached the cave, Valdez led the way, her hand resting on the holster of her gun, poised for any unexpected danger. The temperature inside the cave was considerably cooler than the scorching desert outside, providing momentary relief from the heat.

"Look," Sandra whispered, shining her flashlight on remnants of a makeshift campsite. A tattered sleeping bag lay discarded on the floor, alongside an empty water bottle and some scattered food wrappers.

"Someone's definitely been here recently," Valdez murmured, her eyes scanning the area for any personal belongings or clues that could provide insight into the kidnapper's identity or motives.

"Whoever it is, they're not here now," Nick commented, frustration evident in his voice.

"True." Valdez nodded, kneeling down to examine the sleeping bag. "But we might still find something useful."

"Like what?" Sandra asked, her voice quivering with barely contained emotion.

"Anything that might tell us who this person is or why they took Jamie." Valdez frowned, her mind racing as she tried to piece together the puzzle before them.

"Could this be where they're keeping him?" Nick suggested, hope creeping into his voice.

"Maybe," Valdez replied, trying to keep her tone neutral. She knew how important it was for the family to maintain their hope, but she also didn't want to give them false expectations. "But we need to keep searching, just in case."

"Right," Sandra agreed, wiping away a tear that threatened to fall. "We can't give up on him."

"Never," Valdez assured her, standing up and holstering her gun. "Let's move on. We'll find Jamie. I promise."

As they left the cave, Valdez couldn't help but feel the weight of that promise bearing down on her shoulders. They were closer than ever to finding Jamie, but there was still so much uncertainty. One thing was for sure: they wouldn't rest until they'd brought him home, safe and sound.

The dim light from Valdez's flashlight cast eerie shadows on the cave walls as she continued to search for clues. Nick and Sandra followed closely behind, their eyes scanning every inch of the space.

"Wait," Sandra whispered, her voice barely audible. "What's that?"

Valdez shone her flashlight on a section of the cave wall that appeared slightly different from the rest – a small, almost imperceptible gap between the rocks. She approached it cautiously, reaching out to touch the cool stone surface.

"Help me with this," she said to Nick, who immediately moved to assist her. Together, they managed to pry the hidden compartment open, revealing a stash of newspaper clippings and photographs inside.

"Look at this," Nick said, his voice trembling as he held up one of the clippings. "It's about the missing boys."

"Jesus," Valdez muttered, studying the other clippings and photographs. "This is definitely the kidnapper's lair." She couldn't help but feel a chill run down her spine at the thought of being so close to the person responsible for Jamie's disappearance.

"Nick, look at this," Sandra cried, holding up a book. "Isn't this the same book Jamie was reading in the car?"

"God, you're right!" Nick exclaimed, his face a mix of hope and fear. "We're getting closer."

"Keep your guard up," Valdez warned, knowing the kidnapper could still be nearby. "We don't want to be caught off guard."

"Agreed. Let's keep moving," Nick said, determination etched into his features.

"Where do we go from here?" Sandra asked, her voice wavering as she tried to suppress her growing anxiety.

"Let's follow the trail of evidence from the other two boys," Valdez suggested, her eyes scanning the desert landscape outside the cave entrance. "It might lead us to Jamie."

"Sounds like a plan," Nick nodded, his brow furrowed in concentration.

As they stepped out of the cave and into the vast expanse of the desert, Valdez couldn't help but feel an overwhelming sense of responsibility for the Harris family. She had to find Jamie – not just for their sake, but for her own. The thought of failing them was unbearable.

"Stay close," she cautioned as they began their trek through the unforgiving terrain. "This desert can be treacherous."

"Lead the way, Detective," Sandra replied, her voice filled with renewed determination.

Valdez took a deep breath, steeling herself for whatever lay ahead. She knew that the path to finding Jamie wouldn't be easy, but she was prepared to face any challenge in order to bring him home safely. And with the Harris family by her side, she felt confident they could accomplish anything together.

The sun cast a golden glow on the canyon walls as Valdez led the way, her boots crunching against the gravel beneath her feet. The Harris family followed closely behind, their eyes darting around the treacherous landscape in search of any sign of Jamie or his abductor.

"Are you sure this is the right direction, Detective?" Nick asked, beads of sweat forming on his forehead.

"Based on the evidence we found in that cave, this area seems to be our best bet," Valdez replied, her determination unwavering. "I've got a feeling we're getting close."

"Every second counts," Sandra murmured, her voice strained with worry. "I can't bear the thought of Jamie being out here alone."

"Neither can I," Valdez admitted, her gaze locked on the path ahead. "But we're doing everything we can to find him."

As they navigated the rocky terrain, Valdez couldn't help but marvel at the Harris family's resilience. Despite the oppressive heat and the physical exhaustion of their search, they remained focused on their goal – finding Jamie and bringing him home safely.

"Watch your step here," Valdez cautioned as they approached a particularly precarious section of the canyon. "These rocks can be slippery."

"Thanks for the warning," Sandra replied, gripping her husband's hand for support. "We'll be careful."

"Look!" Suddenly, Sandra pointed to something glinting in the distance, her eyes wide with hope. "What's that?"

Valdez squinted, trying to make out the object through the shimmering heat waves. "It could be something important. Let's check it out."

They hurried towards the source of the glint, their hearts pounding with anticipation. As they drew closer, Valdez felt a knot of anxiety tightening in her stomach. What if this was the break they needed? What if they were finally on the right track?

"Wait," Sandra gasped, her voice choked with emotion as she bent down to inspect a thorny bush. "This... this is Jamie's shirt."

Valdez examined the torn fabric in Sandra's hands, noticing the familiar pattern and color. It was undeniable – they had found a piece of Jamie's clothing.

"Looks like we're on the right path after all," Valdez said softly, her resolve strengthened by this discovery. "We'll find him, Sandra. I promise."

"Thank you, Detective," Sandra replied, tears of gratitude glistening in her eyes. "I don't know what we'd do without you."

"Let's keep moving," Nick urged, his voice thick with determination. "Jamie needs us."

"Right," Valdez agreed, scanning the surrounding area for any more clues. "Stay focused, and stay close. We don't know what we might encounter out here."

As they continued their search, Valdez could feel the weight of responsibility resting heavily on her shoulders. She knew that finding Jamie was not just a matter of saving the boy's life but also of restoring a sense of justice and hope to a family that had been shattered.

With each step they took, Valdez knew they were drawing nearer to their goal. And though the path ahead was uncertain, she refused to let fear or doubt stand in their way. They would find Jamie – no matter what it took.

Valdez's eyes narrowed as she spotted a faint trail of torn fabric leading them further into the canyon. "Look," she said, pointing out the scraps to the Harris family. "We need to follow this path, but we must be cautious. We don't know what's waiting for us up ahead."

"Right," Nick replied, his voice shaky but resolute. "We'll be careful, Detective."

"Let's go," Sandra added, gripping her husband's hand tightly.

Together, they ventured deeper into the canyon, each step taking them closer to the unknown. The narrow path was lined with jagged rocks and treacherous crevices, making their progress slow and painstaking. Valdez took the lead, her every sense attuned to her surroundings, alert for any sign of danger.

"Detective, do you think... do you think Jamie's still alive?" Sandra asked, her voice barely audible over the sound of their footsteps crunching on the rocky ground.

Valdez hesitated, carefully considering her response. She knew that hope could be both a powerful motivator and a cruel tormentor. Finally, she spoke. "I believe there's still a chance, Sandra. And as long as there's a chance, we're not giving up."

"Thank you," Sandra whispered, her eyes filled with gratitude and determination.

As they continued along the path, the air around them grew tense with anticipation. Each member of the group felt the weight of responsibility pressing down on them, driving them forward despite their exhaustion.

"Wait!" Valdez exclaimed suddenly, halting in her tracks. The others stopped as well, their hearts pounding in their chests. "Do you hear that?"

Nick strained his ears, trying to pick up on whatever had caught the detective's attention. "I... I think so. It sounds like... someone crying."

"Could it be Jamie?" Sandra asked, her voice trembling with hope.

"Only one way to find out," Valdez replied, determination etched on her face. "Let's keep moving – but be ready for anything."

With renewed urgency, the family followed the hidden path, their hearts pounding in unison. They knew they were closing in on Jamie's location, and the possibility of a confrontation with his kidnapper loomed large in their minds.

"Stay alert," Valdez warned, her voice low and steady. "We're getting close."

"God, please let him be okay," Sandra prayed silently, her thoughts focused on her missing son.

As they navigated the treacherous terrain, each member of the group was driven by a singular purpose: to find Jamie and bring him home. The fear and uncertainty that had plagued them since the beginning of their search gave way to steely resolve, bolstered by the knowledge that they were closer than ever to reaching their goal.

The sun sank lower in the sky, casting eerie shadows across the canyon as the family emerged from their secret trail. Nick's heart raced with excitement at the sight of the rugged landscape, but his stomach twisted with fear when he saw the daunting cliff that stood before them. It was a sheer drop, plunging into an unknown abyss of sand that seemed to stretch on endlessly. He couldn't help but wonder if they had made a mistake coming here.

"Damn it," Valdez cursed under her breath. "We can't go this way."

"Is there another route?" Sandra asked, her voice tight with frustration and worry.

Valdez studied the landscape, her eyes narrowing as she traced a possible path around the cliff. "Looks like we'll have to circle back and try another approach. It'll take us hours, though."

"Hours?" Nick echoed, despair seeping into his tone. "We don't have hours, Valdez! What if Jamie's—"

"Nick, I know," Valdez interrupted gently, placing a reassuring hand on his shoulder. "But we've come too far to turn back now. We have to keep moving."

"Mom," Lila chimed in softly, tugging at Sandra's arm. "Jamie's strong, right? He'll be okay until we find him... won't he?"

Sandra hesitated, her gaze fixed on the vast expanse of desert before them. She could feel the weight of their situation pressing down on her, but she refused to let fear and doubt consume her. For Jamie's sake – for all their sakes – they had to hold onto hope.

"Of course he will, sweetheart," she whispered, pulling Lila close. "We just have to keep going. We'll find him. We have to."

"Alright, everyone," Valdez announced, her voice carrying a note of authority that seemed to dispel some of the gloom that had settled over the group. "We're losing daylight, so let's move. We'll find another way."

As they turned away from the cliff, Nick couldn't help but steal one last glance at the seemingly endless desert that lay before them. How could they ever hope to find a single person in such a vast, unforgiving wilderness?

"Jamie," he murmured under his breath as if saying his son's name aloud would somehow bring him closer. "Hold on, buddy. We're coming."

As they retraced their steps, the air grew thicker with an oppressive tension. Each member of the family steeled themselves for the next phase of their harrowing journey, determined to find Jamie and bring him home. Their spirits were united by a singular purpose, burning with an unquenchable fire: to rescue Jamie at all costs. They wouldn't rest until they had achieved that goal, no matter what sacrifices they had to make along the way. The thought of failing fueled their determination, pushing them forward with unwavering resolve.

CHAPTER 6

The dimly lit motel room cast eerie shadows on the faces of Detective Valdez and the Harris family as they huddled around a small, rickety table. The tension in the air was thick, each person holding their breath in anticipation. Nick clenched his hands into fists, his knuckles turning white.

"Look at this," Nick whispered, his voice trembling as he held up a scrap of fabric – another piece of Jamie's shirt, similar to the one they found caught on a bush earlier. "I found it... I found it sticking out of the trunk liner of Sheriff Wallace's patrol car."

Detective Valdez leaned forward, her piercing brown eyes studying the torn fabric intently. She reached out a hand to touch it but hesitated, mulling over the implications of this new evidence. Her mind raced, trying to piece together the puzzle before them.

"Are you sure it's Jamie's?" Sandra asked, her eyes wide with fear, hands shaking as she brought them to her mouth. "How did it end up there? What does this mean?"

"Tell us everything, Nick," Valdez said, her voice urgent but steady. "What exactly happened when you found this?"

Nick took a deep breath, steadying himself before recounting the details. "I was walking past the sheriff's office when I noticed his car parked out front. Something just... drew me towards it. When I looked at the trunk, that's when I saw it – just a tiny corner of fabric sticking out from under the liner. It's the same color as Jamie's shirt, and it even has the same pattern."

Valdez rubbed her chin, deep in thought. "This is a significant lead, but we have to be cautious about how we proceed." She glanced around at the anxious faces of the Harris family. "For now, let's keep this information between us. We don't want to tip off Wallace if he's involved."

"Detective, what do we do now?" Sandra pleaded, her voice quivering with a mix of fear and determination. "We can't just sit here and do nothing!"

Valdez's eyes were steely as she made a decision. "I'm going to confront Sheriff Wallace directly. I need all of you to stay here in the motel room while I handle this. Understand?"

The Harris family nodded in agreement; worry etched on their faces. Valdez stood up and took a deep breath, preparing herself for the confrontation ahead. She knew it wouldn't be easy, but the safety of Jamie and the truth behind his disappearance depended on her ability to remain resolute in the face of danger.

As Valdez left the motel room, her steps quick and determined, she couldn't help but wonder how deep the darkness ran within Sheriff Wallace – and whether or not she would be able to bring him to justice. All she could do was forge ahead and hope that the truth would be enough to save Jamie and protect the Harris family from further harm.

Sandra's eyes widened in shock, her breath catching in her throat as she stared at the piece of fabric Nick held between his trembling fingers. For a moment, the dimly lit motel room seemed to fade away, leaving only the chilling realization that Sheriff Wallace was involved in her son's disappearance.

"Is... is this really Jamie's?" Sandra whispered, her hand instinctively reaching out to touch the torn fabric as if the very act could somehow bring her closer to her missing child. Tears welled up in her eyes, the weight of the situation pressing down on her like a physical force.

Valdez clenched her jaw, her face hardening with determination as she absorbed the implications of what lay before them. "It's identical to the piece we found earlier," she said quietly, her mind racing through various scenarios that might explain how the fabric had ended up in the sheriff's patrol car. As much as she wanted to believe it was all a terrible misunderstanding, the evidence pointed to something far more sinister.

"Listen, we can't let anyone know about this yet," Valdez told the Harris family, her voice firm and commanding. "We don't want to tip our hand and risk warning Wallace if he's involved in Jamie's disappearance."

"But what do we do now?" Sandra asked, her voice quivering as she looked at Valdez with pleading eyes. "We can't just sit here and do nothing!"

"Trust me," Valdez reassured her, her gaze never wavering from Sandra's. "I won't rest until we find your son. But for now, we need to keep this quiet. We'll move forward cautiously and make sure we have all the necessary information before we confront Wallace."

As Sandra nodded reluctantly, her hands clenching into fists on her lap, Valdez turned her attention inward, sorting through the swirling thoughts in her head. She knew she had to stay focused despite the growing storm of emotions inside her. If she allowed herself to be swayed by fear or anger, it could jeopardize their chances of finding Jamie and bringing him home safely.

"Things are going to get a lot more dangerous from here on out," Valdez thought, steeling herself for the challenges ahead. "But I won't let this monster win. Jamie deserves justice, and I'll do whatever it takes to ensure he gets it."

Valdez studied Nick's face, searching for any signs of recognition as she asked, "Nick, I need you to think back to when you first met Sheriff Wallace. Did anything seem off or suspicious about him?"

Nick furrowed his brow, his gaze unfocused as he mentally replayed their initial encounter with the sheriff. "I mean, he was definitely intense and serious, but I thought it was just because of the situation," he admitted hesitantly.

"Think harder," Valdez urged her voice firm yet gentle. "Any small detail could be important."

"Alright, there was one thing that seemed a bit odd," Nick said slowly, the memory coming into focus. "When we were talking about Jamie's disappearance, he kept asking about our family, like he wanted to know more about us personally. It didn't really seem relevant at the time, but now that I think about it..."

"Go on," Valdez insisted, her eyes narrowing as she sensed the significance of Nick's words.

"Well, when I mentioned that Jamie loves exploring the woods around our house, I noticed a strange glint in his eyes. It almost looked like... excitement?" Nick's voice trembled slightly, the implications of his observation sending a shiver down his spine.

Sandra's fists clenched tighter, her frustration and anger boiling over. "And what does all this mean? Is that monster responsible for taking my son?" she demanded, her voice quivering with a mix of fear and determination to find Jamie.

"Right now, we can't say for certain," Valdez replied cautiously, her mind racing with the possibilities. "But it's certainly worth looking into further." She locked eyes with Sandra, her voice resolute. "I promise you, we will find Jamie, and if Sheriff Wallace is involved in any way, he'll pay for what he's done."

As Sandra nodded, her eyes glistening with fresh tears, Valdez allowed herself a moment of internal reflection. "I can't let my emotions cloud my judgment," she thought, steeling herself for the difficult road ahead. "But I'll do whatever it takes to bring Jamie back to his family and make sure justice is served."

"Stay here," Valdez commanded, her voice firm yet reassuring. "I'll handle this. I need to confront Sheriff Wallace directly. Don't leave the room until I come back."

Nick and Sandra exchanged a worried glance but nodded their agreement. They knew they had to trust Detective Valdez, for Jamie's sake.

Valdez exited the motel room, her heart pounding in her chest as she strode with purpose toward the sheriff's office. The dark sky overhead seemed to mirror her resolve, the moon casting stark shadows on the ground as she moved briskly, each step fueled by her determination to uncover the truth.

"Focus, Rachel," she thought, her mind racing with possibilities and strategies. "You need to stay calm, keep your cool. You can't let him see you're onto him, not until you have enough evidence."

As she walked, Valdez replayed the conversation she'd just had with Nick and Sandra, analyzing every detail and searching for any clues that could help her build a case against Sheriff Wallace. She knew that confronting him would be risky, but her instincts told her it was the right move. The safety of a child hung in the balance, and she couldn't afford to play it safe this time.

"Remember, Rachel," she reminded herself, "you're doing this for Jamie, for his family. You can't let them down." Her mind swirled with thoughts of confrontation and justice, her steps never faltering in their determined march toward the sheriff's office.

The door to the sheriff's office creaked open, casting a sliver of moonlight across the dimly lit room. Valdez stepped in, her eyes instantly locking onto Sheriff Wallace's cold gaze. He sat behind his cluttered desk, an air of arrogance surrounding him.

"Evening, Detective," he drawled, leaning back in his chair. "What brings you here at this hour?"

"Cut the act, Wallace," Valdez replied, her voice steady and unwavering. She crossed the room, stopping just short of his desk. "I have evidence that you're involved in Jamie Harris's disappearance."

"Is that so?" Wallace sneered, his eyebrows raised in mock surprise. "Well, I'd love to hear what you've got."

"Nick Harris found a piece of Jamie's clothing in the trunk liner of your patrol car," Valdez shot back, watching as Wallace's face briefly flickered with alarm before returning to its smug facade.

"Interesting," he mused. "But that doesn't prove anything. Fabric gets caught up on things all the time. Would you like me to explain how it could've ended up there?"

Valdez's fingers clenched into fists, anger simmering beneath the surface. "I don't need a lesson in forensics, Wallace. What I want is the truth. Where is Jamie?"

"Your guess is as good as mine, Detective." His words were casual, but a barely perceptible tremor ran through them.

"Stop lying!" Valdez shouted, her patience wearing thin. "You know where he is, and I'm not leaving until you tell me!"

"Fine," Wallace sighed, his eyes narrowing into a sinister glare. "You want the truth? You can't handle the truth, Valdez." He chuckled darkly, a sadistic smile playing on his lips. "Jamie's fate is sealed. And you won't find him in time."

"Where is he?" Valdez demanded, her heart pounding in her chest as she envisioned Jamie's terrified face.

"Good luck figuring it out," Wallace taunted, his voice dripping with malice. "You'll need it."

Valdez's eyes bore into Sheriff Wallace, her voice unwavering. "Wallace, we have evidence linking you to Jamie's disappearance. Are you going to tell me where he is, or do I need to bring this to the state police?"

"Ha!" Sheriff Wallace scoffed, his face twisting into a sneer. "You've got nothing on me, Valdez. I have no idea what you're talking about."

"Nothing? Really?" Valdez said, her voice rising in volume as she slammed a hand on the desk between them. "We found another piece of Jamie's clothing in your patrol car. And don't even try to explain it away. You're involved, and you know it."

"Ridiculous," Wallace snapped, his face contorting with anger. "I don't know what kind of game you're playing here, but I won't be a part of it." He turned away from her, feigning indifference.

"Game?" Valdez scoffed in disbelief. "A boy's life is at stake here, you sick bastard! This isn't some petty vendetta; this is about finding Jamie and bringing him home to his family!"

"Detective," Wallace spat, his voice dripping with disdain. "You're grasping at straws. You want me to be guilty so badly that you're willing to fabricate evidence. How pathetic."

Valdez clenched her teeth in frustration, forcing herself to ignore his attempts at deflection. She took a deep breath, trying to maintain control over her emotions. "Listen to me, Wallace. We know you're involved. Just tell us where Jamie is. Please."

"Sorry, Detective," Wallace said with a dismissive wave, his face a mask of defiance. "But I can't help you."

"Fine," Valdez barked, her voice steel. "You want to play games? We'll play games. But remember, Wallace, once this is over, you'll be the one left holding the bag." She shook her head in disgust and stormed out of the office, refusing to let him see that she was shaken by his callous disregard for Jamie's life.

IDENTITY ZERO

As she exited the sheriff's office, Valdez's mind raced with thoughts of how she could break through Wallace's lies and find the truth. No matter what it took, she would not rest until Jamie was found.

Valdez stared intently at Sheriff Wallace, her eyes boring into him as if she could force the truth out of him with sheer willpower alone. The silence in the room grew thick and heavy, the tension almost palpable.

"Fine," she muttered, pulling another piece of evidence from her bag: a photograph of the scrap of Jamie's clothing taken from the trunk liner of Wallace's patrol car. She slammed it down on his desk. "Explain this."

Wallace glanced at the photo, his expression shifting for a moment, betraying a flicker of fear before he quickly masked it again. Valdez caught the change and pressed on, her determination renewed.

"Look at it, Wallace!" she demanded. "That's the same fabric as the piece we found near the bush where Jamie disappeared. This is irrefutable proof that you were there, that you took him!"

Sheriff Wallace hesitated, his resolve wavering. He seemed to struggle internally before finally giving a reluctant admission. His voice was filled with malice as he spoke. "Alright, Detective. You want a clue? Fine, I'll give you one," he sneered, clearly enjoying the torment he was causing. "Jamie's somewhere where the water runs deep and darkness prevails."

"Is that all?" Valdez asked, her frustration boiling over. "You think this is some kind of game?"

"Life's full of games, Detective," Wallace replied, his voice dripping with venom. "Win or lose, it's up to you."

Valdez clenched her fists, her anger barely contained. She wanted nothing more than to wipe the smug grin off of Wallace's face, but she knew that wouldn't help Jamie. Instead, she forced herself to focus on the cryptic clue he had provided, her mind racing through possible locations for the missing boy. As she left the sheriff's office, she vowed to herself and the Harris family that she would uncover the truth and bring Jamie home, no matter what it took.

Valdez stood at the door of the sheriff's office, her hand gripping the handle tightly. She took a deep breath and glanced back at Sheriff Wallace, his mocking grin still plastered across his face.

"Darkness prevails, huh?" she said through gritted teeth. "You're going to regret this, Wallace."

"Like I said, Detective," he retorted, leaning back in his chair, "it's all just a game."

With a final glare, Valdez stormed out of the office, slamming the door behind her. The sound echoed through the empty hallway, mirroring the fury that bubbled within her chest. Her determination was renewed – she would find Jamie, and she would make damn sure that Sheriff Wallace faced the consequences of his actions.

As she marched down the corridor, Valdez replayed the cryptic clue over and over in her head. Darkness prevails... where water runs deep... She wracked her brain for places in the town that fit the description, mentally mapping out the possibilities.

"Think, Rachel, think!" she muttered to herself, her voice barely audible. "Where could he be?"

Her mind raced as she considered various locations – the old quarry filled with rainwater, the underground tunnels beneath the town, the abandoned well on the outskirts. Each seemed plausible, but she knew time was running short. She needed to narrow it down quickly.

"Damn it, Wallace," she whispered, frustration mounting. "Why couldn't you just tell me where he is?"

But deep down, Valdez knew the answer to that question – because he wanted to see her fail. He wanted to see the Harris family crumble under the weight of their grief and desperation. And most of all, he wanted to prove that he held all the power in this twisted game of cat and mouse.

As she stepped out into the fading sunlight, Valdez clenched her fists, her resolve unwavering. She would not let Wallace win; she refused to give him the satisfaction of claiming victory over her and the Harris family. No matter how long it took or what obstacles stood in her way, she would find Jamie and bring him home – safe and sound.

"Let the game begin," she murmured, her voice filled with steely determination as she set off towards the first potential location on her mental list. "I'm coming for you, Jamie."

CHAPTER 7

The dim glow of the setting sun cast long shadows across the cracked asphalt as Valdez and the Harris family stood outside their vehicles, their faces etched with determination. The failed confrontation with Sheriff Wallace had left them more resolute than ever to find Jamie.

"Come on, let's get inside," Nick said, leading the way into a small motel room whose only source of light was a flickering fluorescent bulb overhead. The air inside was stale and heavy, but it was better than standing out in the open where they might be seen.

"Alright, let's put our heads together and figure this out," Valdez said, her voice firm and steady. "What do we know so far?"

"Jamie disappeared from the diner," Sandra started, her eyes filled with worry as she clutched a worn photograph of her son close to her chest. "And we know that Sheriff Wallace is involved somehow."

"Right," Valdez nodded, rubbing her temples as she tried to piece the puzzle together. "We confronted him, but he's still one step ahead of us. We need to find a way to catch him off guard."

"Maybe there's something we missed at the diner," Nick suggested, his brow furrowed in thought. "A clue or... I don't know, anything that could help us figure out where Jamie is."

Valdez considered his words for a moment before responding. "It's possible. But we'll have to be careful. If Wallace is watching us, we don't want to tip him off that we're onto something."

"Agreed," Sandra chimed in, her voice barely audible. "I just want my baby back."

"Hey," Valdez said softly, placing a hand on Sandra's shoulder. "We're going to find him, okay? We won't stop until we do."

"Thank you, Rachel," Sandra whispered, her eyes meeting Valdez's for a brief moment before flicking away.

"Okay, let's get some rest," Nick said, his voice heavy with exhaustion. "We'll head back to the diner first thing in the morning and see if we can find anything."

As they settled into their makeshift beds for the night, Valdez couldn't shake the feeling that they were running out of time. The stakes had never been higher, and she knew that every second counted in their search for Jamie. In the darkness, she silently vowed to herself that she wouldn't let the Harris family down – not when they needed her most.

The first light of dawn crept through the gap in the motel room curtains, casting long shadows on the worn carpet. Valdez, already awake, sipped her lukewarm coffee as she contemplated their next move. Her gaze flicked between Nick and Sandra, who slept fitfully on the lumpy mattress.

"Nick," Valdez said softly, nudging his shoulder. "Sandra. We need to get going."

"Already?" Sandra mumbled, rubbing her eyes. "It feels like we just closed our eyes."

"Time's not on our side," Valdez replied, her voice firm but gentle. "We have to act fast if we want to find Jamie."

"Right," Nick agreed, pushing himself off the bed. "So, what's the plan?"

"Let's go back to the diner," Valdez suggested. "Maybe we missed something, a clue that could lead us to Jamie."

Sandra's eyes lit up with a glimmer of hope. "You think there could be something there?"

"Can't hurt to check," Valdez shrugged. "We don't have much else to go on at this point."

"Okay," Nick nodded, determination etched into his features. "If there's even a chance it'll help us find Jamie, it's worth a shot."

As they gathered their belongings and prepared to leave the motel room, Valdez couldn't help but notice the mixture of hope and anxiety in Nick and Sandra's expressions. She understood their pain – the desperate need for answers and the fear of what they might uncover.

"Remember," Valdez cautioned as they headed towards their car, "we need to be careful. Wallace might still be watching us. Let's try to make this look casual, alright?"

"Understood," Nick said, gripping Sandra's hand tightly.

"Let's do this," Sandra whispered, her voice trembling ever so slightly.

With that, they piled into Valdez's car and set off towards the diner, their hearts heavy with uncertainty but their resolve unwavering. As the miles ticked by, Valdez couldn't shake the nagging feeling in the pit of her stomach – a gut instinct telling her that this was just the beginning of a dangerous game. But for the sake of Jamie and the Harris family, she knew she had to play it through to the end – whatever the cost.

Maggie's face, previously a mask of stoicism, crumbled as she recalled the events surrounding Jamie's disappearance. Her voice trembled as she spoke.

"Th-there was this one man," she began. "Came in shortly after you folks did. Sat at the far end of the counter and didn't order much."

Valdez leaned in, her eyes fixed on Maggie. "Did he interact with anyone?"

"Can't say for sure," Maggie admitted, her brow furrowed with concentration. "But I think he exchanged a few words with that trucker who comes in here all the time. You know, the one with the red cap?"

"Can you recall anything they talked about?" Nick asked, his desperation evident in his voice.

"Sorry, I couldn't hear them over the sound of the coffee machine," Maggie said, shaking her head. "But the man left pretty quickly after."

"Thank you, Maggie. We'll look into it," Valdez replied, her mind already racing to connect the dots.

"Before we go, do you mind if we take a look around outside? Just in case there's something we missed," Sandra asked, her hands fidgeting nervously.

"Of course, go ahead," Maggie nodded, concern etched across her face.

As they stepped out of the diner, the desert sun beat down relentlessly, casting long, distorted shadows on the cracked pavement. They split up to cover more ground, their eyes scanning every inch of the dusty landscape for any clue that could lead them closer to Jamie.

"Valdez!" Sandra called out, her voice wavering. "I found something!"

The detective rushed over, her heart pounding in her chest. Sandra pointed to a set of tire tracks leading away from the back of the diner. The pattern looked recent, with the treads still sharp and defined.

"Could be nothing," Valdez mused, her brow furrowed in thought. "But it's worth checking out."

"Anything that might help us find Jamie is worth checking out," Nick interjected, his eyes filled with determination.

Valdez nodded, a small smile tugging at the corner of her lips. "You're right. Let's follow these tracks and see where they lead."

As they set off to pursue the tire tracks, Valdez couldn't shake the feeling that someone was watching them from afar. She glanced toward Sheriff Wallace's vehicle in the distance, a chill running down her spine.

"Stay alert," she whispered to Nick and Sandra as they walked. "We can't let our guard down."

The wind picked up outside, sending a swirl of dust and debris skittering across the parking lot like tumbleweeds. Inside the diner, Sandra's gaze darted back and forth, her mind racing as she tried to process everything they had learned so far.

"Maybe we missed something," she murmured, more to herself than anyone else.

"Hey, it's possible," Valdez replied, her tone soft and understanding. "Let's give this place another once-over, just to be sure."

As they began retracing their steps through the diner, Sandra couldn't help but feel the weight of their desperate search pressing down on her. Her thoughts were consumed by Jamie, and the fear of never seeing her child again threatened to overwhelm her.

"Focus, Sandra," she told herself, shaking off the wave of panic that threatened to engulf her.

It was then that she noticed something wedged between the cushions of a booth. Her heart skipped a beat as she carefully extracted the torn piece of paper, her hands trembling with anticipation.

"Valdez, look at this!" Sandra called out, barely able to contain her excitement.

The detective hurried over, her eyes narrowing as she read the cryptic message scribbled in hasty handwriting: "Meet me at the old gas station on Route 66. - J."

"Route 66?" Sandra questioned, her heart pounding in her chest. "What could Jamie possibly want us to find there?"

"Good question," Valdez mused, her mind working overtime as she tried to decipher the meaning behind the message. "But it's our only lead so far. We need to check it out."

"Absolutely," Nick chimed in, his voice filled with determination. "We'll follow this lead to the ends of the earth if it means finding Jamie."

"Thank you both," Sandra whispered, her eyes brimming with gratitude. "I couldn't do this without you."

"Hey, we're in this together," Valdez reassured her, placing a comforting hand on Sandra's shoulder. "Now, let's get moving. We've got a gas station to investigate."

As they exited the diner and piled into their vehicles, Sandra couldn't help but feel a spark of hope flickering to life inside her. She knew that finding Jamie wouldn't be easy, but with Valdez and Nick by her side, she felt more determined than ever to bring her child home safely.

The tires of their vehicles screamed against the asphalt as Valdez and the Harris family hurtled down Route 66, the desolate landscape a blur of dust and heat. Their hearts pounded in tandem with the engine's roar, anticipation clawing at their chests.

"Are we sure this is the right place?" Nick shouted over the wind, his knuckles white on the steering wheel.

"Positive," Valdez replied, her eyes fixed on the horizon. "We're almost there. Just keep your eyes peeled for any signs of the gas station."

"I just hope Jamie's okay," Sandra murmured, her gaze distant but focused, as if she could will her son into view through sheer force of will alone.

"Me too, Sandra," Valdez agreed, her voice steady despite the whirlwind of emotions raging within her. This was personal now – not just another case to solve. This was about reuniting a family torn apart by a monster in a sheriff's uniform.

As they rounded a bend, the dilapidated structure of the old gas station finally came into view. It loomed like a ghost from the past, its rusted sign creaking in the desert wind. They parked their vehicles, their engines idling before falling silent. The tension in the air was palpable, thick enough to cut with a knife.

"Here we are," Valdez said, her hand gripping her gun as she stepped out of her car. "Stay close and be ready for anything."

"Let's find our boy," Nick whispered, determination burning fiercely in his eyes. Sandra nodded in agreement, her jaw set with resolve.

As they approached the gas station, Valdez couldn't help but feel a shiver run down her spine. There was something unsettling about the place, as if it had borne witness to unspeakable horrors. But she pushed those thoughts aside, focusing instead on the mission at hand.

"Spread out," she instructed, her voice barely audible. "Look for any signs of Jamie – or anything else that seems out of the ordinary."

As they fanned out, a shadow of doubt crept into Valdez's mind. Was this really the right place? Were they walking into a trap? But she quickly shook off such thoughts, knowing that second-guessing herself would only hinder their search.

"Anything?" Nick called out after several minutes of fruitless searching.

"Nothing yet," Sandra replied, frustration evident in her voice.

"Keep looking," Valdez urged, refusing to accept defeat. "We'll find him. We have to."

The door to the gas station groaned on its rusted hinges as Valdez pushed it open, revealing a dimly lit interior shrouded in dust and decay. Stepping inside, her gun held firmly in front of her; she could feel the weight of the silence pressing down upon them. She turned to Nick and Sandra, who followed close behind, their expressions a mixture of hope and fear.

"Stay alert," she whispered, her eyes scanning the room. "We don't know what we might find here."

"Understood," Nick replied, his voice hushed but steady.

Valdez led the way, carefully navigating around broken glass and debris, mindful of any potential hazards. The air was thick with dust, making it difficult to breathe, and the distant howl of the wind outside only heightened the eerie atmosphere.

"Feels like this place has been abandoned for years," Sandra murmured.

"Probably has," Valdez agreed, her attention focused on the task at hand. "Keep your eyes open for anything that might be a clue."

As they searched, Valdez's piercing brown eyes caught a glimmer of something metallic hidden beneath a pile of debris. Her curiosity piqued, she crouched down, carefully removing the rubble surrounding it.

"What is it?" Nick asked, peering over her shoulder.

"Let me see..." Valdez muttered as she finally uncovered the object – a small, tarnished key. Its significance unknown, but it held a sense of promise.

"Could this have something to do with Jamie?" Sandra questioned, her voice wavering with emotion.

"Maybe," Valdez responded thoughtfully, turning the key over in her hand. "We'll keep it just in case." She slipped the key into her pocket, her mind racing with possibilities.

"Rachel," Nick interjected, snapping her out of her thoughts. "Do you think it's safe to keep searching? What if someone's watching us?"

"Nick's right," Sandra chimed in, her voice tense. "Something feels off about this place."

Valdez paused for a moment, her gaze scanning the room once more, considering their concerns. She knew they couldn't afford to overlook anything, but at the same time, she couldn't risk putting them in unnecessary danger.

"Alright," she finally conceded. "We'll do one more sweep and then get out of here. Stay close."

"Got it," Nick agreed, his eyes darting around the room as they resumed their search.

"Please let us find something," Sandra whispered under her breath, her heart heavy with desperation.

As they moved through the gas station, Valdez couldn't help but feel an unsettling sense of urgency, her instincts warning her that time was running out. They needed answers – and they needed them now.

The flickering shadows cast by their flashlights danced upon the decaying walls of the gas station as they prepared to leave, their collective breaths held in anticipation. Valdez's grip tightened on her gun when a sudden noise echoed through the desolate space. It was a low, guttural growl, followed by the sound of something heavy scraping across the floor.

"Did you hear that?" Sandra whispered, her hand instinctively reaching out to grasp Nick's arm, her knuckles turning white from fear.

"Yeah," Nick replied, his voice strained. "It came from over there." He pointed towards the back corner of the gas station, where rows of rusted shelves lay toppled and forgotten.

"Stay behind me," Valdez commanded, her voice steady despite the hammering pulse in her ears. She took the lead, her gun raised and flashlight slicing through the darkness as they followed the unsettling sound.

"Rachel, what do you think it is?" Sandra asked, her voice trembling slightly.

"Can't say for sure yet," Valdez responded, her mind racing with possibilities – an animal, a trap, or perhaps something more sinister. "Just stay close and be ready for anything."

As they crept closer, the growling grew louder, accompanied by labored breathing. Valdez could feel the hairs on the back of her neck stand up, her heart pounding like a war drum inside her chest.

"Maybe we should call for backup?" Nick suggested, his eyes darting around nervously.

"No time," Valdez countered, her determination unwavering. She knew they couldn't afford to wait if Jamie's life was at stake. "We need to see this through."

As they rounded the corner, the source of the noise finally revealed itself. A large dog, its fur matted and snarling teeth bared, stood protectively over a bloodied piece of cloth. Valdez's eyes narrowed as she recognized it – the same cloth she had seen Jamie wearing in a photo provided by the Harris family.

"Easy, boy," Valdez cooed cautiously, her gun still raised but her voice soothing. "We're not here to hurt you."

"Is that... Jamie's?" Sandra asked, her voice barely audible as she stared at the bloodied fabric.

"Looks like it," Valdez replied, her mind racing with questions. What had happened to Jamie? Was he still alive? And what did this dog have to do with it?

"Rachel, we have to find him," Sandra pleaded, tears welling up in her eyes. "Please..."

Valdez looked back at the Harris couple, their faces etched with desperation and fear. She took a deep breath, steeling herself for the challenges that lay ahead.

"We will," she vowed, her voice firm with resolve. "I promise."

CHAPTER 8

A neon sign flickered above the entrance to the Lucky Motel, casting an eerie glow over the dusty parking lot. Nick rubbed the back of his neck, feeling the grit and sweat cling to his skin as he squinted at the windowless façade. The place looked like it hadn't been updated since the 70s, the paint peeling in long, curling strips. He sighed heavily, his breath catching in his throat as he tried to shake off the unease that settled over him.

"Alright, everyone," Nick said, forcing a smile. "Let's go check-in."

Sandra climbed out of the car, her eyes weary but determined as she took in their surroundings. Valdez followed suit, her gaze sharp and alert as they made their way into the dimly lit lobby.

"Stay close," Nick murmured to Sandra, his hand brushing against hers for a brief moment before he approached the front desk.

"Evening," the man behind the counter greeted them, his tone flat and disinterested. "Got a reservation?"

"Two rooms, please," Nick replied, trying to keep his voice steady as he glanced back at Sandra and Valdez who were scanning the area, their eyes darting nervously.

"Names?" the man asked, his fingers hovering over the keyboard.

"Nick Harris and... Rachel Valdez," he replied.

"Alright, I got you down for two rooms." The man handed Nick two key cards. "Room 108 and Room 109."

"Thank you," Nick said, pocketing the keys and turning back to his family. "We're all set."

"Good," Valdez nodded, her eyes never leaving the door as if expecting trouble to walk through at any moment. "Let's get settled in."

"Are we safe here, Nick?" Sandra whispered, her knuckles whitening around the strap of her purse.

"Let's hope so," he replied, his voice barely audible. In his mind, he couldn't help but wonder if they were truly safe anywhere anymore.

"Come on, let's get to our rooms," Valdez urged, her eyes meeting Nick's for a brief moment, sharing the weight of their mission.

Together, they walked back through the lobby, each step echoing in the silence as they tried to shake off the feeling that they were being watched.

The sound of footsteps filled the room as a motel employee appeared from behind a door marked 'Staff Only.' His eyes locked onto the Harris family and Valdez, his gaze narrowing as he studied them intently. Nick felt his heart rate quicken, acutely aware of the man's piercing scrutiny.

"Hey, Mike," the man at the front desk called to the employee, "can you give these folks a hand with their bags?"

"Sure thing," Mike replied, his voice laden with suspicion. He sauntered over to the family, his eyes never leaving their faces.

"Thanks, but we can manage," Nick said firmly, gripping the handles of their luggage tighter.

"Suit yourself," Mike shrugged, an unreadable expression on his face. He lingered for a moment longer before turning away, disappearing back into the staff-only area.

"Creepy guy," Sandra muttered under her breath as Valdez shot her a concerned glance.

"Stay sharp," Valdez warned, the urgency in her tone unmistakable. "We don't know who we can trust."

"Let's get to our rooms," Nick said, leading the way outside. The desert air was cool against their skin, offering a brief respite from the stifling tension that clung to them like a second skin.

"Room 108 for you, Valdez," Nick handed her one of the key cards. "And Room 109 for us."

"Got it," Valdez acknowledged, her gaze scanning their surroundings, ever vigilant.

"Let's get some rest," Valdez said. "Tomorrow's going to be a long day."

"Goodnight," Nick called as they entered their respective rooms, the doors clicking shut behind them. Inside, he couldn't shake the feeling that the walls were closing in, the weight of their situation bearing down on them.

"We'll find out what happened," he whispered to himself, trying to stave off the creeping dread. "We have to."

Sandra's fingers trembled as she locked the door behind them, her heart pounding in her chest. The room's musty scent and peeling wallpaper only heightened her sense of unease. She moved to the windows, methodically checking each lock and drawing the curtains tight.

Across the way, Valdez had transformed the small table in her room into a makeshift command center, maps and case files spread out before her like puzzle pieces waiting to be assembled. Her eyes darted from one document to another, searching for any clue that might lead them to the truth.

"Anything yet, Valdez?" Nick asked as he and Sandra entered the room, their faces etched with worry.

"Nothing concrete," Valdez admitted, her frustration evident. "But I have a few leads we can follow up on tomorrow."

"Good," Sandra said, forcing a smile. "We'll do whatever it takes to get to the bottom of this."

"I know," Valdez nodded, meeting her gaze. "We're in this together."

"Thank you," Sandra whispered, feeling a renewed sense of determination take hold. "We won't let whoever is responsible for this get away with it."

"Damn right," Nick chimed in, his voice firm. "Let's go over these leads, then get some rest. We'll need our strength for tomorrow."

"Agreed," Valdez said, gesturing for them to gather around the table. "Now, let's get to work."

Nick's heavy footsteps echoed in the small motel room as he paced back and forth, the worn carpet beneath his feet doing little to muffle the sound. His frustration was palpable, each step like a physical manifestation of the pressure bearing down on him. Sandra couldn't blame him; she felt it, too.

"Damn it," Nick muttered under his breath, running a hand through his short, dark hair. "We're running out of time."

Sandra watched her husband for a moment, her heart aching at the sight of his distress. Unable to sit still herself, she began organizing their belongings, her hands trembling slightly as she tried to maintain a sense of control amidst the chaos. She focused on the task at hand, folding clothes and arranging toiletries in neat rows, trying to create some semblance of order.

"Nick, we'll find Jamie," she said softly, pausing her movements for a moment to offer him a reassuring smile. "Valdez is working on those leads. We just have to trust her."

"I know, Sandra," Nick replied, his voice strained. "It's just... every minute that goes by feels like an eternity."

"Believe me, I feel the same way," Sandra admitted, resuming her organizing. "But we can't let our fear control us. We need to stay focused."

"Right," Nick sighed, halting his pacing. He took a deep breath and rubbed his face, willing himself to calm down. "You're right. We've got to keep our heads clear if we want to find our boy."

"Exactly," Sandra agreed, zipping up their suitcase with a sense of finality. "Now, why don't you sit down and take a break? We both need to be ready for whatever tomorrow brings."

For the first time since they had arrived at the seedy Lucky Motel, Nick let out a small, humorless chuckle. "I never thought I'd see the day when you'd tell me to take a break."

"Desperate times, huh?" Sandra replied with a weak smile.

"Desperate times," Nick echoed, finally sinking into one of the room's threadbare chairs. He leaned forward, elbows on his knees, and buried his face in his hands. "We'll find him, Sandra. We have to."

"We will," she said firmly, her voice full of conviction. "Together."

As they sat there in the dimly-lit motel room, the weight of their situation pressing down on them, Nick and Sandra drew strength from each other, ready to face whatever challenges lay ahead in their quest to bring Jamie home.

The flickering neon light from the motel sign outside cast eerie shadows across the room, highlighting the creases of worry etched on Nick and Sandra's faces. Valdez stood in the doorway, her gaze darting between the couple as she sensed the thick tension in the air.

"Hey," she said softly, drawing their attention. "I know this is tough, but we need to stay focused. We're here for Jamie, remember?"

Nick nodded, his jaw clenched. "Of course, we haven't forgotten."

"Then let's use our energy wisely," Valdez suggested, stepping fully into the room. "Arguing or worrying won't bring him back any faster."

Sandra wiped her eyes, taking a shaky breath. "You're right, Rachel. We need to be strong for him."

"Exactly." Valdez moved toward the small table where her makeshift command center was set up. "We're going to find him, I promise you that. But we have to work together."

As they gathered around the table, eyes scanning the maps and case files, the deep silence in the room was suddenly shattered by the distant wail of a siren. All three froze, their hearts pounding in their chests.

"Is that...?" Sandra whispered her voice tight with fear.

"Shh," Valdez cautioned, straining to listen. "Just wait."

As the siren faded into the night, leaving them in a heavy silence once more, Valdez exhaled slowly. "It's gone, for now. But it's a reminder that we need to be cautious."

"Right," Nick agreed, his hands balled into fists at his sides. "We can't let our guard down, not even for a second."

"Let's get to work then," Valdez urged, her focus returning to the task at hand. "We'll go over everything one more time, and then we'll start searching."

Together, they delved into the case files, their determination burning brighter with each passing minute. They were united in their mission to find Jamie and bring him home, no matter what it took.

"Alright, listen up," Valdez said firmly, her piercing brown eyes scanning the faces of Nick and Sandra. "We need to cover more ground if we want to find Jamie faster. I suggest we split up."

"Split up?" Sandra's voice wavered, a hint of concern in her eyes.

"Trust me, it's for the best," Valdez assured them. "Nick, you and Sandra search the immediate vicinity of the motel. Look for anything suspicious, especially any signs of Sheriff Wallace. I'll investigate the nearby establishments for leads."

Nick exchanged an apprehensive glance with Sandra before nodding in agreement. "Okay, let's do it."

With their flashlights in hand, Nick and Sandra stepped out into the desert night, the cool air prickling their skin as they began their search. The darkness felt suffocating, but the beams of their flashlights sliced through it, creating islands of light amidst the shadows.

"Stay close," Nick whispered, his protective instincts kicking in. Sandra nodded, gripping her flashlight tighter.

As they moved cautiously through the surrounding area, Nick couldn't help but feel uneasy. *What if the Sheriff is watching us?* he thought, his heart pounding in his chest. *We can't let him get to Jamie.*

"Nick," Sandra murmured, drawing his attention back to the present. "Over there, by that bush. Do you see something?"

Nick squinted, trying to discern what had caught Sandra's eye. "I'm not sure. Let's check it out."

As they approached, Nick realized it was just a discarded soda can, its metallic surface gleaming in the flashlight's beam. He sighed in frustration, his hope deflating slightly.

"False alarm," he muttered, glancing over at Sandra. "Let's keep moving."

"Wait," Sandra said, the tremor in her voice betraying her fear. "Do you hear that?"

Nick paused, straining to listen. He could barely make out the sound of a car engine in the distance. *Could it be the Sheriff?* he wondered, his heart racing once again.

"Let's get back to the motel," he urged, grabbing Sandra's hand and leading her away from the noise. "We've done all we can for now."

As they made their way back, Nick hoped Valdez had found something more promising. Jamie's safety was all that mattered, and he knew they wouldn't rest until they had brought him home.

Nick's flashlight beam illuminated a dirty, neon-lit sign that read "Pete's Roadhouse" as he and Sandra approached the ramshackle bar. The raucous laughter of patrons spilled from the open doorway, along with the faint smell of stale beer and cigarette smoke.

"Maybe someone in there knows something," Nick suggested, trying to sound more confident than he felt. Sandra nodded, her eyes wide and alert as they stepped inside.

"Hey!" a burly man at the bar bellowed over the noise, his gaze narrowing on Nick and Sandra. "Who're you two lookin' for?"

"Uh, we're just..." Nick hesitated, glancing at Sandra before speaking up. "We're looking for our son. He's gone missing."

"Missing, huh?" the man sneered, swaying slightly as he leaned against the bar. "Well, good luck with that."

"Thanks," Sandra replied tersely, scanning the room for anyone who might be more willing to help.

"Excuse me," she said, approaching a woman nursing a drink in the corner. "Have you seen a boy around here? Fourteen years old, blonde hair, blue eyes?"

"Can't say I have," the woman murmured, taking a sip of her whiskey. "But then again, I ain't been payin' much attention."

"Please," Nick implored, desperation creeping into his voice. "If you know anything, we need to find him."

"Alright, alright," the woman sighed. "I think I saw someone like that earlier today, but I can't be sure. You should ask old Pete over there by the jukebox. He knows everyone around these parts."

"Thank you," Sandra whispered gratefully, making her way toward Pete with Nick close behind.

Meanwhile, Valdez's sharp eyes scanned the faces of the motel staff as she questioned them about any unusual activity or suspicious characters. Her investigative instincts were on high alert, searching for that one detail that might lead her to Jamie.

"Look," the nervous housekeeper confessed, wringing her hands. "I saw a man talking to a boy yesterday. They were in a hurry, and the boy looked like what you described."

"Can you describe this man?" Valdez pressed, her heart pounding with anticipation.

"Um, tall, broad-shouldered, dark hair," the housekeeper stammered. "He had a tattoo on his neck. I think it was a snake?"

"Thank you," Valdez said sincerely, scribbling down the information in her notepad. "This could be important."

As she left the motel, Valdez continued her investigation, stopping by each neighboring establishment with the same set of questions. Each new lead brought her closer to solving the puzzle of Jamie's disappearance, and she refused to let anything stand in her way.

We're going to find you, Jamie, she thought determinedly. *I promise.*

Nick and Sandra trudged back to the Lucky Motel, their clothes damp with sweat and their faces etched with exhaustion. The desert night had offered them little but scorching heat and an ever-growing sense of dread.

"God, I hope Valdez had better luck than we did," Nick muttered, rubbing at his stubble-roughened jaw. He hated feeling so helpless, unable to protect his family, unable even to find his missing son. *Come on, Jamie,* he thought desperately. *Just give us a sign.*

"Me too, honey," Sandra agreed, looping her arm through her husband's. She could feel the weight of their shared fear pressing down on her chest, making it difficult to breathe. "We'll find him. We have to."

As they approached the motel, Valdez appeared in the dim glow of the parking lot lights, her face animated and her eyes alight with determination. "I found something!" she called out as soon as she saw them.

"Please tell me it's about Jamie," Sandra pleaded, her voice trembling with hope.

"Actually, yes," Valdez confirmed, her words tumbled out in her excitement. "One of the witnesses I talked to saw a boy matching Jamie's description being taken into a suspicious-looking vehicle transferred from the Sheriff's police car. The Sheriff and another man were working together. The witness thought Jamie was being arrested."

"Are you serious?" Nick asked, his heart pounding in his chest. "Why would the Sheriff be involved?"

"I don't know," Valdez admitted, "but it's our first solid lead. We need to follow up on this."

"Absolutely," Sandra agreed, her gaze steely. "We'll do whatever it takes to bring our boy home."

"Listen," Valdez said, her voice turning gentle. "I know you two are exhausted, but we need to act fast. I suggest we gather our things and leave this place immediately."

"Right," Nick nodded, a newfound determination settling in. "We don't have any time to waste."

As they hurried back to their rooms to pack, Valdez couldn't help but marvel at the strength and resilience of the Harris family. *They're not going to give up,* she realized. *And neither will I.*

Together, they formed an unbreakable bond, their hope rekindled by the witness's account. With fierce resolve, they set out into the night, ready to follow the new lead and do whatever it took to bring Jamie back home.

CHAPTER 9

The sun dipped below the horizon, casting long shadows across the dusty floor of the sheriff's office as Deputy Sam Rodriguez stood at the entrance, his hand hesitating over the doorknob. A nagging sensation gnawed at him - something was wrong with this case, and he couldn't shake the feeling that Sheriff Wallace was involved in Jamie's disappearance.

Sam took a deep breath and entered the dimly lit room, his eyes scanning for any signs of evidence that might connect the sheriff to the crime. He moved cautiously, acutely aware of the creaking floorboards beneath his feet. The last thing he needed was for anyone to catch him snooping around.

"Alright, Sam, think," he whispered to himself. "If there's anything here incriminating the sheriff, where would it be?"

His heart raced as he rifled through filing cabinets, looking for any irregularities or hidden compartments. All the while, his mind kept replaying images of Jamie, the lanky teenager with curly blonde hair who loved music, and the pained expressions on his parents' faces. They deserved answers, and Sam was determined to find them.

"Come on, come on," he muttered, growing more frantic as he searched. Then, just as he was about to give up, he noticed an inconspicuous file tucked away at the back of a drawer. It seemed out of place amidst the otherwise orderly system.

"Jackpot," he whispered, pulling the file out and carefully examining its contents.

Sam's hands shook as he read through the pages, his eyes widening with each passing moment. The file contained records of Sheriff Wallace's frequent meetings with a man named Rankin. As he dug deeper, it became clear that Rankin was running a human trafficking ring, kidnapping young kids and transporting them to Los Angeles before taking them overseas to sell.

"God, no," Sam breathed, his stomach churning at the horrifying realization. "That's why that man was seen transferring Jamie from the sheriff's car."

He could hardly believe it - his mentor and role model, entangled in such a heinous operation. Sam's heart pounded in his chest as the gravity of the situation sank in. He knew he had to act, but he couldn't face this alone.

"Alright, Sam, get it together," he told himself. "You need help. Detective Valdez and the Harris family deserve to know the truth."

With the incriminating file tucked under his arm, Sam turned to leave the office. As the door creaked shut behind him, he steeled himself for what was to come. His once unwavering loyalty to Sheriff Wallace had been shattered, replaced with an unyielding determination to bring the truth to light and rescue Jamie from the clutches of those who sought to harm him.

Under the dim glow of a flickering streetlight, Sam Rodriguez paced nervously. He clutched the hidden file to his chest as if it were his lifeline. The remote location he had chosen for the meeting was an old, abandoned gas station on the outskirts of town. Abandoned vehicles and debris littered the area, casting eerie shadows in the moonlight.

"Come on, Valdez," Sam muttered under his breath, glancing at his watch. "We don't have much time."

Finally, a set of headlights pierced through the darkness, approaching the gas station. As the car came to a stop, Detective Rachel Valdez stepped out, her expression tense and alert.

"Rodriguez?" She called out, squinting into the darkness.

"Over here, detective," Sam replied, emerging from the shadows.

Valdez approached him cautiously. "What's going on? You sounded urgent on the phone."

"Detective, I've discovered something... something horrible." Sam hesitated for a moment, struggling to find the courage to reveal the truth. "I found this hidden file in Sheriff Wallace's office."

"Wallace?" Valdez raised an eyebrow as she took the file from him, flipping through the pages. Her eyes widened with each chilling revelation, disbelief etched across her face. "You're sure about this?"

"Positive. Rankin is running a human trafficking ring, and it appears that Sheriff Wallace is involved. That's how Jamie got mixed up in all of this."

Valdez closed the file; her jaw clenched, anger simmering beneath her stoic exterior. "This is monstrous. We need to get this information to the Harris family immediately. They deserve to know what we're up against."

"Agreed," Sam nodded, relief washing over him as he realized Valdez was on his side. "We can't trust anyone else in the department."

"Alright, here's what we'll do," Valdez said, her mind racing as she formulated a plan. "We'll meet with the Harris family tonight and share everything we've learned. We'll need to be careful, though – if Wallace finds out we're onto him, he might try to cover his tracks."

"Understood. I'll contact the Harrises and set up a private meeting at their home. They should be safe there," Sam suggested.

"Good. Do that," Valdez agreed. "And Rodriguez... be careful. If Wallace realizes you know something, it could put you in danger."

"Thank you, Detective. I'll be cautious." With that, they parted ways, each feeling the weight of responsibility on their shoulders as they prepared to face the dark truth head-on.

The moon cast a faint glow over the remote location, providing just enough light for Sam Rodriguez to recognize the figures approaching. Nick and Sandra Harris walked cautiously toward him, their eyes darting around as if expecting danger to lurk in every shadow. Detective Valdez followed closely behind, her focused gaze sweeping over the area.

"Thank you all for coming," Sam whispered, his voice barely audible against the night's silence. "I have some information that could help us find Jamie."

"Please, tell us everything," Sandra urged, desperation etched on her face as she clung to Nick's arm for support.

"Alright," Sam began, his voice hushed as he relayed the evidence he had uncovered. "I found a hidden file in the sheriff's office. It contained records of Sheriff Wallace's meetings with a man named Rankin. Turns out Rankin runs a human trafficking ring, and they've been kidnapping kids and transporting them to Los Angeles before sending them overseas." He hesitated, glancing at the distraught parents. "I believe this is how Jamie got involved." The two kids that were found dead must have attempted to escape.

"Are you saying our son has been kidnapped by traffickers?" Nick asked, his voice trembling with fear and anger.

"Unfortunately, it seems that way," Sam replied solemnly. "But there's more. The records show that they may be temporarily storing the kids in an abandoned mine shaft nearby. I think that could be our connection to Jamie's disappearance."

Detective Valdez took control of the conversation, her experience showing through. "We need to investigate this mine shaft discreetly. If we can find proof of their operation, we'll have the evidence needed to bring down Wallace and Rankin."

"Anything to get our boy back," Nick said, determination seeping into his voice.

Sandra glanced between Sam and Valdez, her maternal instincts taking over. "What do we do next? How do we proceed without putting Jamie or ourselves in more danger?"

"First, we need to gather our equipment and plan our approach. We don't know what kind of security measures they have in place," Valdez advised.

As they discussed their next steps, Sam couldn't help but feel a sense of camaraderie with the Harris family. Their dedication to finding Jamie at all costs mirrored his own desire for justice. He knew that together, they could face whatever darkness awaited them in the abandoned mine shaft.

"Let's bring our boy home," Nick whispered, determination etched on his face, as the group prepared to embark on their dangerous mission.

The sun dipped below the horizon, casting long shadows across the dusty landscape as Detective Valdez studied the topographical map of the area surrounding the abandoned mine shaft. Her thoughts raced with the implications of what they might find there, and she knew that every decision she made could mean the difference between life and death for Jamie.

"Alright," she said, her voice steady and focused. "We'll split into two teams to cover more ground. Nick and I will approach from the east while Sandra and Sam take the west. We'll maintain radio contact at all times but keep it to a minimum to avoid detection."

Nick nodded, his face etched with determination. "Understood. What's our rendezvous point?"

"Let's meet at this clearing" – Valdez pointed to a spot on the map – "about a quarter-mile south of the mine entrance. It should provide enough cover for us to regroup without being seen."

"Sounds like a plan," Sandra replied, her voice laced with both fear and resolve. She glanced at Sam, who tried to offer a reassuring smile despite his own anxieties.

"Remember," Valdez continued, "our priority is ensuring everyone's safety. If you encounter any trouble, don't hesitate to call for backup. We're in this together."

With that, they each grabbed their gear and prepared to set out on their separate paths. As they moved through the fading twilight, Valdez couldn't help but replay their earlier conversation in her mind.

Is Jamie really down there? And if he is, what hell has he been put through?

"Stay focused, Rachel," she muttered under her breath, forcing herself to concentrate on the task at hand.

As they neared the rendezvous point, Valdez signaled for Nick to halt. Crouching behind a large boulder, she scanned the area with her binoculars, ensuring that no unwelcome eyes were watching them.

"Looks clear," she whispered, motioning for Nick to follow her. "Let's meet up with the others."

Together, they crept through the underbrush, their hearts pounding in anticipation of what they might discover within the mine shaft's depths. When they finally reached the clearing, Sandra and Sam were already waiting, their faces grim but resolute.

"Everyone ready?" Valdez asked, her voice barely above a whisper.

"Ready as we'll ever be," Nick replied, his eyes locked on the dark entrance to the mine that loomed ahead.

"Then let's go find Jamie," Valdez said, taking a deep breath as they stepped forward into the unknown.

The moon cast a faint, eerie glow on the dense forest floor as Valdez and the Harris family approached Rodriguez, who stood near their meeting spot with a backpack of supplies. The chilling atmosphere mirrored the anxiety that gripped them all, but there was no turning back; they needed to find Jamie.

"Got everything?" Valdez asked Rodriguez, her tone urgent but hushed.

"Flashlights, maps, walkie-talkies, extra batteries... I think we're set," he replied, his youthful face lined with worry.

"Good job," Sandra whispered, her voice laced with gratitude, as Nick nodded in agreement. They were all aware of the risks Rodriguez was taking by helping them.

"Listen up," Valdez said, taking charge. "We need to move quickly and quietly. If anyone spots us, we're screwed."

"Understood," Nick replied, his athletic frame tense with determination. He'd do whatever it took to protect his family.

"Let's stick together. And remember..." Valdez paused, locking eyes with each of them. "No heroics. We don't know what we're walking into, so stay alert. If something goes wrong, use the walkie-talkies to communicate."

"Or scream," Sam added, trying to lighten the mood. His attempt at humor fell flat, but his bravery and loyalty were evident.

"Let's do this," Sandra whispered, her maternal instincts driving her forward.

With flashlights in hand, the group set off toward the abandoned mine shaft. Valdez led the way, using her detective skills to navigate the treacherous terrain. The darkness seemed to close in around them, but they pressed on, their determination unwavering.

Damn it, Jamie, you better be alive, Valdez thought, her heart pounding in her chest. She couldn't shake the image of the boy's frightened face, and the thought of him falling prey to human traffickers sickened her.

"Valdez, wait," Rodriguez whispered, his brow furrowed. "I think I see something up ahead."

"What is it?" she asked, her voice tense.

"Looks like tire tracks," Nick said, kneeling down beside Rodriguez to inspect the ground. "Could be a vehicle was here recently."

"Or a trap," Sandra interjected, her fear for Jamie's safety overriding any semblance of optimism.

"Only one way to find out," Valdez said, steeling herself for whatever lay ahead. "Let's keep moving."

As they continued their trek through the dark forest, each member of the group grappled with their own thoughts and fears. But beneath it all, one thing remained constant: their unwavering determination to rescue Jamie from the clutches of evil.

The moon cast a ghostly glow over the mine shaft's entrance, shrouded by shadows and overgrown foliage. It seemed to beckon them, ominously urging them forward. The group huddled together, their breaths shallow and quiet.

"Stay low and keep your eyes open," Valdez instructed, her voice barely above a whisper. "We don't know what kind of traps or surveillance Wallace might have set up."

"Got it," Rodriguez replied, his eyes darting around as he clutched the flashlight tightly in his hand.

"Jamie... hang on, please," Sandra murmured, her heartache palpable in her voice.

Valdez led the group towards the mine shaft, her senses heightened with each step. They moved cautiously, scanning the area for any signs of danger. The adrenaline coursing through their veins made for a potent cocktail of fear and determination.

"Look, there's a security camera," Nick pointed out, his voice low and urgent. "We need to disable it."

"Leave that to me," Rodriguez said, pulling out a small device from his pocket. Within moments, the camera was rendered useless, allowing them to proceed without leaving a trail.

"Nice work," Valdez praised him, her focus never wavering from their mission.

"Anything for Jamie," Rodriguez replied, his resolve evident in his tone.

As they reached the mine shaft's entrance, Valdez paused and surveyed the area. "Keep a lookout while I search for any clues or signs of recent activity," she instructed.

"Is there anything specific we should look for?" Sandra asked, her maternal instincts driving her to be as proactive as possible.

"Footprints, discarded items, anything that could point us to Jamie," Valdez answered, her eyes already searching the ground around them.

"Over here!" Nick called out suddenly. "I've found something."

The group rushed over to where Nick was kneeling, a small piece of fabric clutched in his hand. "It's from Jamie's jacket," Sandra whispered, tears welling up in her eyes.

"Let's hope it's a sign that he's still alive," Valdez said, her determination renewed by this small yet significant discovery.

"Come on, let's keep moving," Rodriguez urged, the weight of their mission pressing heavily on his shoulders.

As they ventured further into the mine shaft, their flashlight beams slicing through the darkness, Valdez couldn't help but feel a mixture of fear and hope. *We're coming for you, Jamie,* she thought, her resolve unwavering. *And we won't stop until we find you.*

The beam of Valdez's flashlight flickered across the rocky walls, casting elongated shadows that seemed to reach out for them as they ventured deeper into the mine shaft. The air was thick with dust, and the silence was punctuated only by their echoing footsteps.

"Stay close," Valdez whispered to the group, her eyes narrowed in concentration. "And keep your ears open for anything unusual."

"Got it," Rodriguez replied, his voice barely audible as he followed closely behind her.

As they continued to navigate the dark tunnel, Sandra clutched her husband's arm, fear gnawing at her insides. "Do you think we're getting closer?" she asked, her voice trembling.

"Hard to say," Nick answered quietly, his gaze locked on Valdez's back. "But we have to keep going."

"Rachel," Rodriguez called out, using her first name to emphasize the urgency in his voice. "I think I hear something."

Valdez halted in her tracks and strained her ears, listening intently. After a moment, a faint sound registered – muffled cries, distant and desperate. Her heart pounded in her chest. "You're right, Sam. This way."

"Please let it be Jamie," Sandra whispered, tears stinging her eyes.

"Stay alert," Valdez reminded them as they picked up their pace, driven by the growing sense of urgency. "We don't know what we could be walking into."

"Or who," Nick added darkly.

As they rounded a bend in the tunnel, Valdez's flashlight illuminated a fissure in the wall. It looked like any other crack, but something caught her eye – a small, almost imperceptible lever hidden within the shadows.

"Wait," she said, motioning for the others to stop. "I think I've found something."

"What is it?" Rodriguez asked, peering over her shoulder.

"Look," Valdez said, pointing to the lever. "This might be our way in."

"Only one way to find out," Nick muttered.

Valdez reached out and pulled the lever, her muscles tensed in anticipation. The sound of grinding stone filled their ears as a hidden door slowly opened before them, revealing a concealed chamber.

"Unbelievable," Rodriguez breathed, his eyes wide with shock.

"Quickly, let's go," Valdez urged, leading them into the room. The muffled cries grew louder, worming their way into their hearts and minds.

"Jamie!" Sandra called out, her voice raw with desperation. "We're here!"

"Stay focused," Valdez reminded them, her own fear threatening to bubble over. "And be ready for anything."

Valdez's heart pounded in her chest as she took the first step into the hidden room, her flashlight cutting through the darkness like a knife. Sandra followed closely behind, gripping her husband's arm for support, while Rodriguez brought up the rear, his hand resting on the holster of his service weapon.

"Be ready," Valdez whispered, her eyes scanning every inch of the dimly lit chamber. It was difficult to discern much, with shadows clinging to every corner and crevice, but she could make out rows of caged cells lining the walls. The cries were louder now, each one a dagger to her soul.

"Jamie!" Sandra cried out, the waver in her voice betraying her fear.

"Mom?" A weak response came from one of the cells, and Nick's face contorted with a mix of relief and fury.

"Stay calm, Jamie," Valdez urged, her words directed at both the boy and his parents. "We're going to get you out of here." Her mind raced with questions - how many kids had been held captive in this hellish place? And more importantly, where was Sheriff Wallace?

"Detective Valdez," Rodriguez said shakily, swallowing hard as he stared at an ominous-looking door at the far end of the room. "Do you think...?"

"Wallace might be in there," she finished for him, her voice hardening with resolve. "We need to confront him, but we have to be smart about it."

"Let's free Jamie and any others first," Nick insisted, his eyes never leaving his son.

"Agreed," Valdez said, directing Rodriguez to help with the locks. As they worked, she allowed herself a moment to breathe, her thoughts racing. _How had Wallace managed to hide this operation for so long? And what would they find behind that door?_ She pushed the questions aside; they needed to focus on rescuing the children first.

"Got it!" Rodriguez exclaimed as the lock clicked open. Sandra rushed forward, pulling Jamie into a tight embrace, tears streaming down her face.

"Are you okay?" Nick asked his son, his voice thick with emotion.

"Y-yeah, Dad," Jamie stammered, clinging to his mother.

"Everyone, stay close," Valdez ordered, her eyes locked onto the ominous door. "We're going to confront Wallace, and we need to be prepared for anything."

"Ready," Nick said, determination etched into his features. Rodriguez nodded, his grip on his weapon tightening.

"Let's do this," Valdez whispered, leading the way towards the door, every step bringing them closer to the sadistic sheriff who had orchestrated this nightmare. Her mind raced, formulating strategies and contingencies, but she knew that, ultimately, they would have to face whatever lay behind that door head-on. There was no turning back now.

Valdez's hand hovered over the door handle, her heart pounding in anticipation of what lay beyond. With a deep breath, she pushed the door open, revealing a dimly lit corridor lined with more cells. At the far end stood Sheriff Wallace, a twisted smile playing on his lips as he watched their approach.

"Well, well, well," Wallace drawled, his voice dripping with malice. "I was wondering when you'd show up, Detective Valdez. And you've brought some company." His gaze flickered over the group, his eyes lingering on Jamie cowering behind his parents.

"What is this sick game you've been playing, Wallace?" Valdez demanded, her voice steady despite the rage simmering beneath the surface.

"Game? Oh no, Detective. This is far more than just a game," Wallace sneered, stepping forward to meet them. "This is about power, control, and the thrill of watching those weaker than me suffer."

At that moment, a team of FBI arrived, taking Wallace into custody.

"You won't get away with this," Valdez stated firmly, her grip on her weapon unwavering as the FBI agents restrained Sheriff Wallace.

Other children rescued from the cells were ushered out by medical personnel while the team secured the area. Valdez felt a mix of relief and anger as she watched the perpetrator being taken away, his smirk now wiped clean off his face.

Nick put a reassuring hand on Valdez's shoulder, wordlessly acknowledging the intense emotions swirling within her. Sandra held onto Jamie tightly, grateful to have him back in her arms.

As the commotion settled down, Deputy Rodriguez approached Valdez tentatively. "I... I had no idea, Detective. I didn't know what he was really capable of."

Valdez regarded him with a mixture of understanding and resolve. "You couldn't have known, Sam. But now you do. We have to ensure that justice is served for all those affected by Wallace's cruelty."

CHAPTER 10

Days later. Sam's hands trembled slightly as he straightened the stack of note cards on the lectern. The room was filled with an uneasy anticipation that seemed to weigh down on his shoulders like a lead blanket. He could feel the eyes of the small crowd gathered in the sheriff's office, each one eagerly awaiting his first words as the newly appointed sheriff.

"Uh, hello, everyone." Sam cleared his throat, trying to project confidence he didn't quite feel. "Thank you all for being here today."

A few nods and murmurs of encouragement from the audience helped calm his nerves a bit. He glanced at the first card, took a deep breath, and began to speak.

"First of all, I'd like to express my deepest gratitude for the opportunity to serve as your sheriff," said Sam, his voice gaining strength. "I know this position comes with great responsibility, and I promise you that I will do everything in my power to uphold justice and protect our community."

"Good on you, Deputy—uh, Sheriff Rodriguez!" called out an older man from the back of the room. A ripple of laughter spread through the crowd, and Sam couldn't help but smile, feeling a newfound sense of camaraderie with these people he had sworn to serve.

"Thank you, Mr. Thompson," Sam replied, chuckling along with them before continuing. "In light of recent events, I think it's crucial that we address the elephant in the room. As many of you know, Sheriff Daniel Wallace has been arrested, and I can assure you, he will no longer be able to hurt anyone again."

The room fell silent for a moment, the gravity of the announcement sinking in. Then, a woman near the front stood up and asked, "What are you going to do differently, Sheriff Rodriguez? How can we trust you won't turn out like him?"

Sam felt a knot forming in his stomach as he faced the question head-on. Wallace had been his mentor, and he had trusted him implicitly. But now, that trust had been shattered by the horrifying truth. He needed to show these people that he was not Wallace and that he would never become like him.

"Ma'am, I understand your concerns," Sam answered sincerely, meeting her gaze. "I want you all to know that my commitment to this community goes beyond just catching criminals and keeping the peace. I will work tirelessly to rebuild the trust that has been lost, and I will make sure that our office is a shining example of integrity and transparency."

As Sam spoke, he could see the woman nodding slowly, along with several others in the crowd. They seemed willing to give him a chance, and that meant everything to him. Although he knew the road ahead would be difficult, Sam felt a renewed sense of purpose and determination.

"Thank you for your faith in me," he said, his voice full of genuine emotion. "Together, we'll move forward and ensure that Elk County remains a safe and prosperous place for us all."

The applause rang in Sam's ears like a triumphant anthem, the weight of responsibility settling on his shoulders. He watched as the Mayor approached him, his eyes narrowed, and lips stretched into a forced smile.

"Congratulations, Sheriff Rodriguez," the Mayor said through gritted teeth, extending his hand.

"Thank you, sir," Sam replied, shaking the Mayor's hand firmly. A part of him could sense the reluctance behind the gesture, but he knew that earning the trust of everyone would take time.

As the crowd began to disperse, Sam caught sight of Detective Valdez stepping outside the sheriff's office with the Harris family. Their faces were a mixture of relief and sadness, a testament to the ordeal they had endured together.

"Rachel," Nick called out, his voice strained with emotion. "We can't thank you enough for everything you've done for us."

Valdez smiled warmly, her eyes glistening with unshed tears. "I was just doing my job, Nick. But I'm glad I could be there for your family when you needed it the most."

"Your dedication meant the world to us," Sandra added, grasping Valdez's hand tightly. "You didn't give up, even when things seemed hopeless."

"Mom's right," Jamie chimed in, his voice still slightly shaky from his injuries. "You're like a superhero, Detective Valdez."

Valdez laughed softly, brushing away a tear that had escaped down her cheek. "I'm no superhero, Jamie. Just a cop who cares deeply about justice and the people she serves."

"Still," Nick insisted, "you went above and beyond the call of duty. We'll never forget what you did for us."

As the Harris family exchanged heartfelt goodbyes with Valdez, Sam couldn't help but feel a surge of pride in his fellow officer. She embodied the values that he wanted their department to stand for: integrity, dedication, and compassion.

"Rachel," Sam called out to Valdez, catching her attention. "You did an outstanding job on this case. I want you to know that as sheriff, I'll always have your back."

"Thank you, Sam," Valdez replied with a grateful nod. "I know you'll make a great sheriff."

Sam watched as the Harris family walked away, their shoulders squared with newfound resilience. He knew they still had a long road ahead of them, but he couldn't help but feel hopeful for their future. And in that moment, he made a silent vow to himself: he would do everything in his power to ensure that Elk County was a safe haven for families like the Harrises, free from the shadows of corruption and violence that had once plagued it.

The sun dipped low in the sky, casting a warm glow over Elk County as the Harris family reluctantly climbed into their car. The dull thud of the doors closing echoed their mixed feelings – relief at leaving the ordeal behind and sadness at saying goodbye to their newfound friends.

"Ready, guys?" Nick asked, his hand gripping the steering wheel tightly. Sandra and Jamie exchanged a glance before nodding.

"Ready," Sandra replied, her voice steady but tinged with emotion.

As they pulled away from the sheriff's office, Nick focused on the road ahead, but his thoughts were consumed by the harrowing events that had transpired. He couldn't help but wonder how different their lives would be now.

"Hey, Dad?" Jamie's tentative voice broke through Nick's reverie.

"Yeah, buddy?"

"Can we... can we listen to some music? You know, like we used to do on our trips?" There was a certain vulnerability in Jamie's request – a longing for normalcy and comfort in the familiar.

"Of course," Nick said softly, his fingers reaching for the radio dial. As the strains of a classic rock tune filled the car, he caught Sandra's eye in the rearview mirror. She smiled and squeezed Jamie's hand, offering reassurance.

"Mom, did you ever think something like this could happen to us?" Jamie asked hesitantly, his eyes never leaving his mother's.

"Jamie, no one could have predicted this," Sandra replied gently. "But what's important is that we faced it together, and we came out stronger."

"Damn right," Nick interjected, glancing at his wife and son. "You two showed incredible strength and courage through all of this." He paused, reflecting on the harrowing ordeal they had endured. "I'm so proud of both of you."

"Thanks, Dad," Jamie murmured while Sandra gave Nick a grateful smile.

As they drove out of Elk County, the sun dipped below the horizon, and the first stars began to appear in the indigo sky. The car hummed along the highway, carrying the Harris family away from their past and toward an uncertain future.

"Nick?" Sandra's voice was quiet but determined. "Whatever happens next, we'll face it together, right?"

"Absolutely," he replied without hesitation, his hand finding hers and giving it a reassuring squeeze. "We've got this."

"Yep," Jamie chimed in, his voice filled with newfound resolve. "We're unstoppable now."

The highway stretched out before them, a seemingly endless ribbon of gray cutting through the vast desert landscape. As the last remnants of

Elk County disappeared in the rearview mirror, the silence inside the car grew heavier, suffocating.

"Are you okay, sweetheart?" Sandra asked Jamie, her voice barely more than a whisper.

"Uh-huh," he muttered, staring blankly at the passing scenery.

The silence resumed, interrupted only by the hum of the engine and the occasional gust of wind buffeting the car. Lost in their own thoughts, memories of their harrowing experience washed over them like a tidal wave – the kidnapping, the fear, the desperation to survive.

Sandra's mind replayed the moment when Sheriff Wallace had threatened her family, his eyes cold and merciless. The terror she felt then still lingered a phantom sensation that made her shudder involuntarily.

"Mom, will things ever be normal again?" Jamie's question broke through the quiet, his voice heavy with concern.

"Normal is what we make it, Jamie," Sandra replied, turning to face him. "We can't change what happened, but we can choose how we move forward from it."

Nick nodded, his grip on the steering wheel tightening. "Your mom's right. We've been through hell, but that doesn't mean it has to define us."

"Exactly," Sandra said, her voice filled with determination. "We'll rebuild our lives, stronger than before. We won't let this break us."

For a moment, the three of them shared a knowing glance, each understanding the weight of their words. Their ordeal had tested them beyond measure, but they had emerged from it united and unbroken.

"Promise me something," Sandra continued, her gaze fixed on her husband and son. "Promise me that we'll always stand together, no matter what life throws at us."

"We promise, Mom," Jamie answered without hesitation, his voice steadier than before.

"Always," Nick echoed, the conviction in his voice leaving no room for doubt. Together, they would face the challenges ahead, refusing to let their traumatic past define their future.

As the sun dipped below the horizon, casting a golden glow over the skyline, the Harris family approached their familiar Chicago neighborhood, the sight offering a sense of comfort and normalcy after their ordeal. The rhythmic hum of traffic, the laughter of children playing in the park, and the faint smell of freshly baked bread from the bakery down the street enveloped them like a warm embrace.

"Home," Nick whispered, his eyes taking in the familiar surroundings with a newfound appreciation for life's simple pleasures.

"Finally," Sandra replied, reaching over to squeeze her husband's hand. "It feels like we've been gone forever."

Jamie, still recovering from his injuries, gazed out the window, his eyes filled with a newfound resilience. "We did it, didn't we? We made it through all that...and now we're back."

"We are," Sandra confirmed, turning to face her son. "And we're going to make the most of this second chance."

"Here we are," Nick announced as he pulled into their driveway, the engine purring to a stop. He exchanged a glance with Sandra, their eyes conveying a silent understanding: things would never be quite the same again, but they could learn to live with that.

"Let's go inside," Jamie suggested, unbuckling his seatbelt and wincing slightly as he moved his arm. "I want to see if everything's still how we left it."

"Good idea," Sandra agreed, opening the car door and stepping out onto the pavement. "I'm sure it'll feel strange at first, but we need to start getting used to being home again."

Nick frowned in thought, his mind racing with the challenges ahead. "We can do this, right? I mean, we've come so far already..."

"Of course we can, Dad," Jamie reassured him, his voice brimming with determination. "We've faced worse, haven't we?"

"Jamie's right," Sandra chimed in, her gaze locked on Nick. "We're stronger than we've ever been before. And we have each other."

"Alright then, let's do this," Nick said, his voice firm with resolve. He opened the front door, and they stepped into their home, eager to begin the next chapter of their lives together.

"Welcome home, Harris family," Sandra declared, her words echoing through the once-familiar space. "This is where our new journey begins."

Nick opened a cardboard box labeled "KITCHEN" in bold, black letters. He pulled out a frying pan and set it on the counter, feeling a small sense of comfort in the simple act. The familiar clang of pots and pans brought back memories of countless meals prepared in this kitchen, where laughter and love had once filled the air.

"Hey, I found my old headphones!" Jamie exclaimed, his voice muffled by a mouthful of bubble wrap. "I thought we'd lost these."

Sandra smiled as she unwrapped a treasured family photo. "It's funny how being away from home can make you miss the little things, isn't it?"

"Absolutely," Nick agreed, taking a moment to glance around the room, letting the familiarity wash over him. "You don't realize what you have until it's gone."

"Speaking of which," Sandra said, her voice suddenly serious, "we have our first therapy session tomorrow. Individually and then as a family. Do you think... do you think it'll help us?"

Nick hesitated, unsure of how to answer. He knew they needed professional help to process the trauma they'd experienced, but at the same time, he couldn't shake a lingering fear that it would only dredge up painful memories. "I hope so," he finally admitted. "But we won't know until we try."

"True," Sandra sighed, gently placing the photo on the mantel. "I just want us to be okay again, you know?"

"Me too," Nick murmured, squeezing her hand reassuringly. "We'll get there, one step at a time."

Over the following weeks, the Harris family immersed themselves in therapy sessions. They spoke honestly about their fears, their pain, and the challenges they faced in moving forward. It was difficult to confront the demons that haunted them, but with each conversation, they found themselves growing stronger, more resilient.

"Dr. Patel said that it's important for us to communicate openly," Sandra shared one evening after a family session. "We can't expect to heal if we're bottling everything up."

"Agreed," Nick nodded, taking a deep breath before sharing his own thoughts. "I've been feeling... angry lately. Not at you guys, but at what happened to us. And I'm scared that anger will consume me if I don't learn how to let it go."

"Mom, Dad," Jamie interjected, his eyes glistening with unshed tears, "I've been having nightmares. I know I shouldn't be afraid anymore, but sometimes... sometimes the darkness just feels like it's closing in."

"Thank you for telling us, Jamie," Sandra replied softly, pulling her son into a warm embrace. "We'll work through this together. As a family."

As they unpacked their belongings and settled back into their old routines, the Harris family began to rediscover the solace that their home once offered. Each day brought new challenges but also new opportunities to grow and heal.

"Slowly but surely, we're finding our way back," Nick mused one night as they sat down to dinner, a simple meal prepared with love.

"Back to the people we were before?" Sandra asked, raising an eyebrow.

"No," he replied thoughtfully, meeting her gaze. "Not exactly. But maybe... maybe to something even better."

Under a clear blue sky, the Harris family trudged up a steep hill, the sound of crunching leaves underfoot and Jamie's laughter filling the air. Nick led the way, his muscular form casting a long shadow on the path ahead, while Sandra followed closely behind, her eyes glued to their son as he raced ahead with newfound energy.

"Wait up, Jamie!" Nick called out, feigning exhaustion. "You're too fast for your old man!"

"Can't catch me!" Jamie shouted back, grinning from ear to ear as he crested the hill.

"Careful, kiddo," Sandra warned gently, her voice tinged with the ever-present fear that still lingered beneath the surface.

"Mom, I'm okay," Jamie reassured her, his blue eyes meeting hers with a tender understanding. "We're all okay now."

"Speaking of being okay," Nick interjected, wiping the sweat from his brow, "I think it's time we introduced some fun into our lives again. What do you say we have a game night tonight? Just like old times."

"Sounds great, Dad!" Jamie agreed enthusiastically, the prospect of laughter and friendly competition sparking a light in his eyes.

"Alright then, it's settled," Sandra smiled, her heart swelling with love for her resilient family.

That evening, the Harris dining table was transformed into a battleground, littered with board games, playing cards, and snacks. As they played, the family engaged in open and honest conversations about their shared experiences, creating an atmosphere of healing and understanding.

"Hey, guys," Jamie said hesitantly, pausing between moves in their heated game of Monopoly. "I just wanted to say... thank you. For never giving up on me. For always being there."

"Of course, sweetheart," Sandra replied, reaching across the table to squeeze her son's hand. "We're a family, and that means we face everything together."

"Besides," Nick added with a grin, "we wouldn't be the same without you. You're our rockstar."

Jamie chuckled at his father's praise, his cheeks flushing a deep shade of red. "I guess what I'm trying to say is... I'm not scared anymore."

"Good," Sandra said softly, her eyes shimmering with unshed tears. "Because neither are we."

As time passed, the Harris family continued to engage in activities that promoted healing and bonding. Family hikes became a weekend ritual, game nights a much-anticipated event, and heart-to-heart conversations a daily occurrence.

With each new experience, the scars of their ordeal began to fade, replaced by a newfound strength and resilience that they carried with them. Life would never be the same as it was before their harrowing journey, but perhaps that was for the best. Together, they were stronger than ever before, and nothing would ever break their bond again.

The sunlight poured through the living room window, casting a warm glow on the Harris family as they settled into their seats, preparing for their weekly movie night. Nick pressed play on the remote, and Sandra handed out bowls of popcorn to Jamie and herself.

"Remember when we used to take evenings like this for granted?" Sandra mused aloud, her eyes reflecting the dancing light from the screen.

"Feels like a lifetime ago," Nick replied, his arm wrapping around her shoulders. "But it's brought us closer than ever."

"Definitely," Jamie chimed in between mouthfuls of popcorn. "I never thought I'd say this, but I kinda... appreciate everything now."

Nick laughed, ruffling Jamie's curly hair affectionately. "That's my boy."

As the movie played on, the family exchanged light-hearted banter, enjoying each other's company and savoring the simple pleasure of being together. In the midst of the laughter, Sandra caught Nick's eye, her gaze filled with gratitude and understanding.

"Hey, Dad," Jamie said, pausing the movie. "Do you think we'll ever be able to forget what happened?"

"Maybe not entirely," Nick admitted, rubbing his chin thoughtfully. "But we don't have to let it define us, either. We've come out of it stronger, more resilient, and with a deeper appreciation for life. That's something we can carry forward."

"Your father's right," Sandra agreed, her voice steady and determined. "It wasn't easy, and we'll always have those memories, but we're moving forward together."

Jamie nodded, his eyes shining with a newfound strength. "You know what? You're right. We survived, and we're stronger for it."

"Exactly," Nick said, smiling proudly at his son. "We've got each other, and that's all that matters."

"Alright, enough talking," Sandra declared playfully, reaching for the remote. "Let's get back to the movie."

"Deal," Jamie agreed with a grin, sinking back into his seat as the film resumed.

As the night wore on, the Harris family laughed and cried together, their bond stronger than ever before. Their harrowing desert odyssey had forever changed them, but it had also given them an unshakeable appreciation for life and each other. And with that newfound strength, they were ready to face whatever the future held, united as one.

About the Author

Brian Leslie is a Nationally Recognized Coercive Interrogation Expert and Best Selling Author. He is regularly retained by Federal, State, and Military Courts on high-profile murder cases throughout the United States.

Read more at https://www.brianleslieauthor.com.

About the Publisher

As a boutique book publisher, we take on only a few new authors per year. We focus on building an author's brand, thereby directing more resources towards their overall success. Authors accepted by True American Publishing become creative partners, therefore, participating in their own success.

Printed in the USA
CPSIA information can be obtained
at www.ICGtesting.com
JSHW022059120524
62808JS00001B/19